The Wizard Islands

Jane Yolen

The Wizard Islands

Illustrated by Robert Quackenbush

Includes photographs, old documents, and maps

Thomas Y. Crowell Company • New York

DESIGNED BY ROBERT QUACKENBUSH

Manufactured in the United States of America

The publisher thanks the following for granting permission to use pictures from their collections:

The Bettmann Archive for the pictures on pages 34 and 68.
Erna R. Eisendrath for the photograph on page 70.
Icelandic Airlines for the photograph on page 100.
Iceland Tourist Bureau for the photograph on page 104.
The New York Public Library for the pictures on pages 12, 18, 22, 41, 45, 47, 62, 71, 90, 96.
Rand McNally & Co., Chicago, for the photographs on pages 56, 59, 60, 64. From *Aku, Aku* by Thor Heyerdahl. Copyright 1958 by Thor Heyerdahl. Published in the United States by Rand McNally & Co.
Viking Press, New York for the illustration on page 88, reproduced from *No Longer on the Map* by Raymond H. Ramsay.
Wide World Photos for the photographs on pages 72 and 103.

Library of Congress Cataloging in Publication Data

Yolen, Jane H
  The wizard islands.

  SUMMARY: Includes tales, true and legendary, of various new and ancient islands throughout the world.
  [1. Islands—Fiction] I. Quackenbush, Robert M., illus. II. Title.
PZ7.Y78Wh   [Fic]   73-4474
ISBN 0-690-89671-9

10 9 8 7 6 5 4 3 2 1

This book is for
all the Stemples:
David, Heidi, Adam, and Jason,
Fritz and Betty Lee (and Lisa),
Bill and Dottie and John
Bob, Ionia, and Kristy Ann
Dick and Liz and Lara
and in memory of
Elizabeth Wilber Stemple

Special thanks to my cousin, Captain Freddy Yolen, for his help in finding these islands on the charts of the world; to Raine Bennett of the Islands Research Foundation who started me on my island-hopping years ago; and to Marilyn Marlow, Ann Beneduce, and my husband David Stemple for encouragement along the way.

Contents

. . . past the setting of the sun
To wizard islands, of august surprise . . .

—Vachel Lindsay
from *Litany of the Heroes*

FOREWORD

Islands can be found everywhere—in oceans, seas, bays, gulfs, lakes, and rivers. There are well over one hundred thousand islands on our planet.

Some of these islands are so small, a single tree could not grow on them. Some of these islands are so large, they hold an entire population of people.

Some of these islands are so old, they still use the ancient spellings: eland, ealond, ilond, illond, yllonde, ylond, ylande, hylyn. Some of the islands are so new, they arose from the ocean floor only yesterday.

And almost every one of these islands has a singular tale attached to it.

This is a book about island tales. Certainly there are not a hundred thousand tales in this book. But these are the tales of the islands that interested me the most: islands of magic, islands of mystery, islands where strange things still happen and ghosts still tread the shores, islands where scientists and scholars have found true mysteries even more fascinating than fictional ones.

Loren Eiseley has written that "Voyages without islands to touch upon would be epics of monotony." Let this book be the start of a voyage for you, a voyage filled with stops at wizard islands of august surprise.

Jane Yolen
Phoenix Farm
Hatfield, Massachusetts

The Wizard Islands

Ghost Islands

Ghost Islands

At the time of World War II, a group of scientists and sociologists made the first really comprehensive study of all of the world's islands. It was undertaken because islands were very important to the strategy of the War, especially in the Pacific. But legends and stories about islands had been told and retold for thousands of years before the fact-gatherers got around to studying islands seriously. And many of those legends and stories were about ghosts.

Here are the strange stories of six islands that hold nine ghosts.

Chapter 1

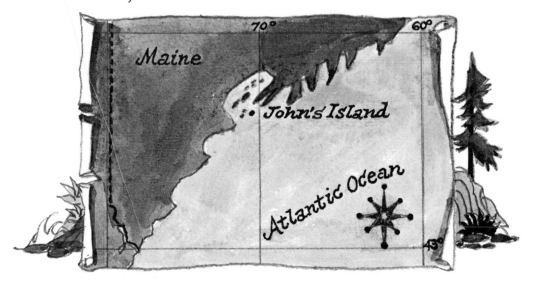

JOHN'S ISLAND
Latitude: 43° 41' N
Longitude: 70° 18' W

The Ghostly Guardian

Casco Bay is one of two great natural divisions in the Maine coast. It is shaped like a skull and was called Bahia de Casco, Bay of the Skull, by the sixteenth-century Spaniard who discovered it.

Many islands dot the blue waters of Casco Bay, riding like a small fleet at anchor in its cold waters. There are so many of them that they are called the Calendar Islands, for supposedly there are 365 of them, one for each day of the year.

One of the smaller islands in the skull is John's Island. It is an ordinary island except for one thing. There is a ghostly guardian that will let no one near the pirate treasure that lies at the bottom of a deep well.

In the 1650s there was a tavern on the north end of

the island. It was a frame house that was visited regularly by the coastal sailors. No one, it was said, was ever refused a drink at the bar. And many a New England sailor spent his shore leave—and his pay—at the tavern on John's Island.

One of the regulars was a wizened, pock-marked sailor known as Portuguese Joe. Whenever Portuguese Joe arrived, he came with pockets full of silver and gold coins. It was obvious he was no ordinary sailor, for the amount of money he carried at each voyage's end was far too vast for any regular seaman. Word soon got around that Joe was a crewman on a pirate ship. They said he sailed with Dixie Bull, the infamous Maine pirate.

Whenever he returned to John's Island, Portuguese Joe always asked for the same room at the inn. The room overlooked the channel that separated John's Island from the mainland. It was whispered that Joe kept an eye out for the troopers.

One day, far away from Maine, in a foreign port, Portuguese Joe lay dying. The only one in the room with him was his current drinking companion. Joe signaled his friend to the bedside. He slipped his hand under the pillow and drew out a folded, dirty piece of paper.

"That's John's Island," Joe said to his friend in a harsh whisper. "Follow the mark and in the bottom of the well you will find more gold and silver than you can carry."

The friend took the paper from the dying man and held it under the flickering candle. "So, you really *were* a pirate," he said.

"With Dixie Bull," Joe whispered. "I helped bury the gold and silver there." He coughed violently. "It was from our ship the *Dare Devil*."

His friend looked up from the map. "You think it's still there?" he asked.

But Joe didn't answer. Instead he whispered "Go only

at night." Then he coughed violently twice and died.

The next day, Joe's friend hastily left the inn where they had been staying. He didn't even bother to arrange for poor Joe's burial. He had taken another look at the map, showing the southern end of John's Island and what looked like a tree and an arrowhead pointing to a clump of rocks near a bank of earth covering an old well. Dixie Bull's treasure! He must get there before anyone else.

But it was nearly six months before he could get back to New England. And three more before he managed to get to Casco Bay. Along the way, he scraped up an acquaintance with another sailor. One night, when the two were drinking, he told his friend about Portuguese Joe.

His friend laughed. "Do you believe that rot?"

"Do I believe it?" He reached into his jumper and brought out a worn leather pouch. Untying the leather string, he repeated, "Do I believe it?" and drew out the map. He unfolded it on the table between them. "What do you see there?"

"John's Island!" said his companion. "But that's right out there." He pointed across the bay.

"Right. And tonight I'm going digging for pirate treasure."

The other man laughed. "And I'm coming along."

"Well, why not," said the first sailor.

Carefully they put the map away and waited until midnight. Each with a spade, they made their way down to the water's edge. They put their tools into a dinghy they had stolen, and rowed quickly, quietly out to John's Island. There was a heavy fog, but they were sailors and used to maneuvering in uncomfortable weather. Soon they landed on John's Island and, within an hour, found the tree and rocks and the bank of earth indicated by the map.

"This is it," whispered one.

They began to dig. Scarcely had one spade been shoved into the bank of earth when there was a loud crash from the cat spruces on the ridge behind them.

Out of the woods galloped a huge black stallion. Even in the fog, they could see the whites of his eyes and his teeth gleaming. His hooves struck sparks whenever they touched rock. He came charging straight at them. The two men dropped their tools and ran for the boat. They rowed madly for the mainland.

The next night they returned. Their tools were right where they had been dropped. But when the men tried to resume their digging, they were driven away again by the stallion.

Two more nights they tried, and each time they scarcely got a spade into the earth before they were frightened away by the wild horse.

They came back the next morning with guns, hoping to shoot the great black horse. But though they found hoofprints, they never could find the animal itself by daylight. And by daylight they also could not find the old well.

They never found the treasure either.

To this day, anyone digging on John's Island at night is chased away by the ghostly stallion, a stallion that legend says bullets cannot kill. Anyone digging by day cannot find Dixie Bull's gold or the spot marked on the treasure map.

And somewhere, I believe, Portuguese Joe is laughing.

Chapter 2

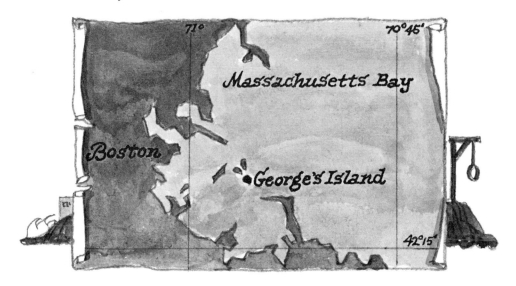

GEORGE'S ISLAND
Latitude: 42° 18′ N
Longitude: 70° 58′ W

The Lady in Black

Along the granite walls of Fort Warren, the island strong-hold that once held over a thousand Confederate prisoners, walks the dark, hooded figure of the Lady in Black. She speaks no words either in anger or in sorrow, but she has haunted the island fortress on George's Island for over a hundred years. Everyone who has seen her in her flowing black robes or watched her ghostly footprints appear in the snow is reminded of her sad tale.

Fort Warren was not originally built as a prison. Con-structed in 1833 on George's Island, seven miles from Boston, it was the center of Boston's seaside defense. The island itself had housed settlers since Puritan days. In fact, its name came from one tenant, John George, who had lived there in the 1700s.

Fort Warren was considered impregnable, with its 248 guns, many of them trained directly on the city itself. Its walls were twelve feet thick, of Quincy granite. By the Civil War, it was such a Northern stronghold, that famous Confederate prisoners like Commissioners James Murray Mason and John Slidell, and even the Confederate Vice-President, Alexander Hamilton Stephens, were incarcerated there. It was the commandant's proud boast that, though one thousand "Rebs" were held there, not one had ever escaped.

But escape attempts were made by the imprisoned rebel soldiers. One of the most daring—and one of the most tragic—was the attempt made by the husband of the girl who became known as the Lady in Black.

A young Confederate soldier by the name of Andrew Lanier, just newly married, was captured in the fighting at Roanoke Island. He was shipped north with his companions to the Boston Harbor prison before word of his capture could be given to his wife. Once in the federal prison, he managed to send a message to his bride through Southern sympathizers living nearby.

His message was simple. He told her that he had been imprisoned in Fort Warren's escape-proof Corridor of Dungeons.

The Corridor of Dungeons. Its dread reputation had penetrated even to the deep South. But the young bride from Crawfordville, Georgia, was determined to rescue her husband. So she found a blockade-runner who agreed, for a price, to take her up the New England coast.

She cut her hair, bought a man's suit and an old pepper-box gun. Then she went on board the blockade-runner's ship disguised as a man. The trip was long. It took two and a half months. But at last one night, she was set ashore on Cape Cod.

The first leg of her journey was over.

At Cape Cod, a Southern sympathizer had been alerted to the girl's arrival and quickly brought her into his home. He found her a clean—though worn—suit and then brought her to the house of yet another rebel friend. This Southerner lived only a mile from George's Island. He was the man who had first smuggled her husband's letter out of Fort Warren.

For more than a week, the girl made her home there. During the day she familiarized herself with the fort through a powerful telescope. She even knew behind which of the fort's windows was her husband's cell. At night she went over her plans.

At the end of a week, a storm blew up in the East, hitting the Boston Harbor islands with great force. It was what they were waiting for. With her host at the oars, the girl was rowed across the waters of Nantasket Road and landed upon the beach at George's Island on January 15, 1862. Then the boat, rowed by her friend, slipped back into the storm again and was lost from sight.

Lying face down in the sand near some shrubs, the girl waited while the patrolling guards went by. She clutched a bundle which held her pepperbox gun and a short-handled pick.

The minute the guards were out of sight, she ran to the walls of the fort.

Under the seven-inch gun slits that were used as windows, she whistled a tune that she and her husband had used as a signal when they were courting. In moments there came an answering whistle. As she watched, a cloth rope made of bedsheets appeared through the slit. She quickly knotted the end around her waist and was pulled up by the prisoners inside. She had only planned to hand the gun and pick through the slit, but she was so slender that she managed to slip through the slit herself. Relief flooded through her. The guards had not seen her. She looked around and, at that moment felt strong arms about her waist—her husband's arms. Their joy at being reunited almost made them forget their danger. But after a loving embrace she pushed him away and handed him the bundle with the pick and gun inside. Her plan, she said, was that they should dig a tunnel out of the fort. The Southern sympathizers, with whom she had stayed, would have a schooner waiting for them every night for a month.

The other prisoners made a tight circle around the girl and her husband. They slapped each other's back, chuckling delightedly at the simplicity of the plan. But one of the rebel lieutenants had a more involved idea.

"We could tunnel to the outer corner and then back into the center of the fort," he said. "That's where the arsenal is. Then we could arm ourselves, and . . ."

Another soldier broke in. "Once we had guns, it would be easy to capture the fort. There are almost a thousand of us. Only eighty Yankees. We could *all* escape."

The lieutenant nodded, shushing the excited men. "But

we won't just escape. We'll turn the big guns on Boston. We'll give the Yankees a real surprise!"

In a hushed, awed voice, the girl said what they were all thinking: "It could change the whole course of the War . . ."

No one slept that night. They stayed up until dawn putting the finishing touches on the lieutenant's plan. Before check-up in the morning, they began the tunnel, covering its mouth with a thin layer of dirt to keep the guards from noticing it. It took great ingenuity to get rid of the dirt they dug out. Sometimes the prisoners even took turns sitting on piles of fresh dirt in order to conceal their activities.

As the weeks went by, the tunnel lengthened. The girl was kept out of sight by the prisoners and fed from their own meager rations. They carried all the extra dirt from the growing tunnel back to the Corridor of Dungeons in their shirt and pants pockets. At night, when the patrolling guards had passed, the men threw some of the dirt out of the window, to be scattered by the steady sea breezes. Some they could stamp into the dirt floor of the basement cells.

Finally the night came when the lieutenant announced that they had tunneled under the parade grounds. By his calculations, they would break through the tunnel top and come out in the arsenal.

At ten o'clock, the Corridor of Dungeons was silent. The men listened intently for the sound of the tunnel's completion. They massed at the tunnel entrance, passing dirt along and scattering it in silence. The lieutenant sent the whispered signal back. "This is it."

With a final swing of the pick, the lieutenant broke through the top. But instead of dirt, his pick smashed against a granite wall. The ringing of the pick on the stone was like the tolling of a death knell.

They had miscalculated badly. The sound of the pick on the granite alerted a Union guard. He shouted a warning down to the sergeant in charge, and the fort was put on instant alert.

Colonel Justin Dimmock, who was in charge of the fort, took several guards with him. They made a fast, surprise visit to the Corridor and found many of the prisoners frantically scattering dirt. But of the tunnel there was no sign.

The guards made a quick search of the cells, but in the dark, with only candles to light their way, they could not find the tunnel they knew must be there. The soldiers finally gave up the search and instead checked their prisoners. One by one, the Southern soldiers were searched, then removed from the Dungeons to a dry moat. When the last prisoner was removed, Colonel Dimmock realized that eleven were still missing. Obviously they were in the elusive tunnel.

At daylight, the guards easily found the tunnel entrance in a corner dungeon.

"We have you," shouted the colonel into the tunnel mouth. "My men are at each end of the tunnel. Come out or be starved out."

Inside the tunnel, the eleven prisoners and the young girl made a hasty plan.

"You all surrender," said the girl, "and then when the soldiers are busy searching you and are sure no one else is missing, I'll surprise them. I'll use old Dimmock as a hostage."

The girl's husband did not like the plan, but he was outvoted. The eleven prisoners filed out of the tunnel's mouth. They were searched roughly, and then Dimmock began to address them, his back to the tunnel.

Just as he began to talk, the girl crept from the tunnel. In a quiet voice she said, "Surrender, sir. I'm quite prepared to shoot."

Casually Dimmock put up his hands. Just as the Southern prisoners started to move towards him and the girl's husband ran towards her side, Dimmock whirled. He knocked the gun to one side. The girl pulled the trigger and the old rusty pepperbox gun exploded. Fragments from the gun flew in all directions. One pierced her husband's brain. He was dead before she could reach him.

The irony of it so stunned the other Confederates that they were quickly recaptured. The girl was taken prisoner, too.

She was sentenced to be hanged as a spy. On the morning of her execution, Colonel Dimmock came to her and asked if she had any final request.

"Please, Colonel, I would like to die in a gown instead of this filthy suit."

The Colonel had the fort searched for something suitable. The only thing resembling a gown was an old black robe that had been worn during a play the cadets had given the summer before.

The girl fashioned a gown out of the black robe and was executed in it on February 2, 1862. She was buried beside her husband in the Fort Warren cemetery.

But that was not the end of the story of the pretty and courageous Southern bride.

Seven weeks after her execution, one of the guards who

View of Fort Warren Boston harbor.

Interior of the Fort.

had witnessed the hanging—Richard Cassidy—was patrolling the area where the girl had died. Jokingly, the other guards warned him to beware of "The Lady in Black." As Cassidy walked his station, he thought about how brave the girl had been even during her last moments. Suddenly he felt two hands around his throat. He turned and was confronted by an apparition in flowing black robes. He ran screaming from the scene. Poor Cassidy was sentenced to thirty days in the guardhouse for leaving his post. His superiors did not believe in ghosts. But Cassidy's successors did.

Since the night young Cassidy ran away from the ghost, the Lady in Black has appeared every year, or at least has made her presence known. Sometimes only her footprints are seen. They have appeared in the snow, small, clear, and feminine, even when it was definitely known that no living woman was on the island.

One sentry who was forced to patrol the execution area went mad.

Another time, in 1947, Captain Charles Norris of Maryland was alone on the island, reading at his post. Someone tapped him on the shoulder. When he turned around, no one was there. He shrugged and went back to his book. Just then, the phone rang, but by the time he answered it, it had stopped. When he picked up the phone, the operator said "Number please?"

Captain Norris said in an agitated manner, "I don't want any number. You called me. Why did you ring?"

The operator answered, "Your wife picked up the phone and took the message."

But Captain Norris did not have a wife on the island. There was no one there but him—and the Lady in Black.

According to people who have visited the island recently, the pretty Southern bride still walks by the granite walls in her long black dress.

Chapter 3

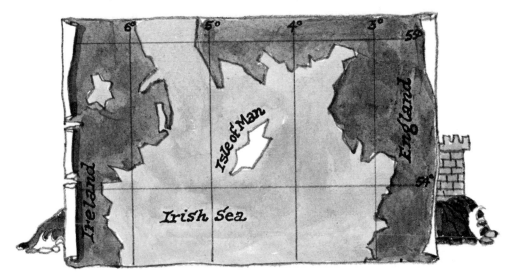

ISLE OF MAN
Latitude: 54° 14' N
Longitude: 4° 9' W

The Dreaded Black Dog

There is a frequent mist that surrounds the lozenge-shaped island in the Irish Sea that is called the Isle of Man. In years gone by, it was said that King Mananaan Mac-y-Lir could call up that fog to make the island vanish whenever an enemy tried to attack. But it has been many long years since anyone tried to attack the island. It is invaded now only by tourists and by fans who come to watch the annual motorcycle and car races.

Still, the fog and mist make the island seem eerie. A visitor might imagine ghosts, spectres, and fairies on his own even if the Manxmen, as the dwellers on the Isle of Man are called, weren't ready to supply such stories. But most Manxmen, like the rest of the Celts, claim to have seen the "little people," and their island is rich in mysterious tales.

The Manxmen tell, for example, of a poor traveler who was led up and down the forest paths for miles by invisible fairie musicians. The poor man could not resist the fairie music. He danced up and down the Manx mountains—some as high as two thousand feet—until at last he came to a common. There he saw a troop of little men feasting and drinking. He thought he recognized some of the faces, but they were so small he wasn't sure.

The fairies invited him to their table. But before he could settle himself on the grass, one of the wee men drew him aside.

"Do not eat or drink," warned the little man, "or you will remain here as one of us. So have I done. So might you."

The poor traveler was not too weary to be wary. He listened to the warning. Though he was given a cup of fine fairie liquor, when no one was watching he threw the wine on the ground. Immediately the music ceased, and the company of fairies disappeared. The traveler found himself alone in the mountain meadow, the cup still in his hand.

He made his way home and went immediately to his minister to tell of his adventure. "And what," he ended his story, "shall I do with the fairie cup?"

"You could do no better than to give it to the church," said the minister.

This cup, it is said, is the chalice that is still used for consecrated wine in Kirk Merlugh.

There are many such stories on the Isle of Man. They are quite similar to tales told in Ireland and Scotland, for the Isle is a Celtic land. The people are of the same background as the Irish and the Scots. But the Manxmen tell one curious story that is totally their own. It is a grim legend of the Mauthe Dhoo, the dreaded black dog that haunts the guardroom of Castle Peel.

Peel sits on a rocky islet. It is a medieval walled fortress, so in effect, it is an island upon an island in an island. The castle was originally made of soft red sandstone. The castle, its walls and fortifications, the gatehouse, and cathedral are all in ruins now. All that has endured is the story of the fearful black dog.

Between the church and castle, there had been a passage that led to the guard chamber. The passageway was closed long before the castle crumbled. The reason for its closing was the Mauthe Dhoo.

The black dog was not a hideous or frightening creature to look at. It was just a large black spaniel with curly, shaggy hair. But it was a ghost dog. It appeared from nowhere, it belonged to no man, and where it went in the daytime when it disappeared from the castle no one could say. No one ever got close enough to pet it or whistle it to his side. The dog had been seen padding through every room in Castle Peel. But the room it was seen in most frequently was the guard chamber. It was always seen in the evening coming out of the passageway that led from the church to the castle guardroom. And before each day dawned, it rose and disappeared back down the corridor whence it came.

Every night, as soon as the candles were lighted, the Mauthe Dhoo would come silently into the guard's apartment and lie down before the fire.

All the soldiers saw it. Though each new recruit was frightened of the spaniel at first, they soon became used to its presence. This did not lessen their real fear, however. The guards were convinced to a man that the dog was evil, and that it was but awaiting permission to do them harm. For this reason, the guards at Castle Peel were abnormally quiet, soft-spoken, and circumspect. They did not swear or joke with one another because of the dog's presence. In fact, the soldiers were so afraid of being alone with the Mauthe Dhoo, that they developed the custom of going everywhere in pairs. The Mauthe Dhoo's passageway was carefully avoided by all.

One night, though, a new recruit had too much to drink. He became very bold and swore that he would walk the passage that night by himself, and see where the Mauthe Dhoo came from.

"I need neither friend nor enemy wi' me," he said in an over loud voice. "I'm no whinin' coward. I'll see that Mauthe Dhoo, be it dog or devil."

The other guards tried to make him change his mind. But the more they said, the more he insisted on going. He even challenged the ghost dog to meet him in the corridor. Then he snatched the keys from the hook upon which

they were hanging, and walked boldly out of the guard-room, down the Mauthe Dhoo's passageway.

No one followed him. No one dared. For surely he had, with his loud, mocking voice, called up the dog—or the devil himself.

It became very quiet in Castle Peel. For some minutes after the young guard had left, the very silence was like a sound.

Suddenly a loud moaning filled the castle. The walls began to echo with loud knocks. Terrifying winds whistled through the halls. And then came a howl. It began on a long low note and rose steadily until the men had to cover their ears for fear their eardrums might burst. It was the howl of a dog—or of a soul in anguish.

Then the sound ended, just as suddenly as it had begun. The soldiers were so frightened they could not move.

In the new silence, another ominous noise began. *Footsteps* were coming slowly along the corridor towards the guardroom.

The soldiers looked at one another in alarm. What could be coming along so slowly, almost dragging its feet?

The door creaked open. It was the young guard returning to the room.

"How goes it?" called out one of his friends.

"What was the noise?" asked another.

Then someone asked the question they were all thinking. "Did ye see it? Did ye see the dog?"

But the young guard did not answer them. He sat down, his eyes staring ahead.

For three days he sat like that, neither talking nor eating nor sleeping. At the end of the three days, he died.

No one ever dared go through the guardroom corridor after that, even by day, and so it was walled up.

And the Mauthe Dhoo was never seen again.

Chapter 4

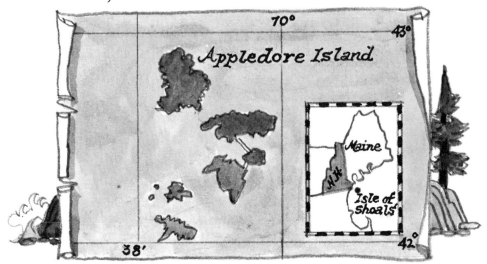

APPLEDORE ISLAND
Latitude: 42° 49′ N
Longitude: 70° 37′ W

The Misnamed Pirate

The Atlantic Ocean is quiet and glassy under a slate grey sky. Far out to sea, a storm is forming. A low undertone, like the mournful cry of wind over the mouth of an empty jar, begins to come from the beach.

"Do you hear Hog Island crying?" asks an old sailor. "Now look out for a storm."

No one knows why Hog Island—now called Appledore —cries before a storm.

And no one knows why the ghost of Philip Babb walks the shingly beach above the cove that bears his name. Some people say he is guarding Captain Kidd's pirate treasure. Others say that Constable Babb is still doing his duty, guarding the shores of the Isles of Shoals as he did before the American Revolution.

There are seven islands in the Isles of Shoals—or eight if

the tide is high, for one of the islands is cut in two by the rising waters. The dividing line between Maine and New Hampshire runs through the middle of the Isles, so that four belong to the former and the other three to the latter state. The islands lie hazy and cloudlike on the Eastern horizon, ten miles out from Portsmouth, New Hampshire, small outposts of rock.

The islands were discovered early in the recorded history of America. Captain John Smith in the first part of the 1700s called them after himself—Smith's Isles. But they soon became known as the Isles of Shoals, not because of the ragged reefs which have wrecked countless ships but because of the "shoaling" or schooling of fish about.

The Isles are wild, weather-torn, and lonely. Little grows on them except blueberry, bayberry, and huckleberry bushes and occasional wild roses. In fact, the treeless rocky islands are ideal for nothing but drying fish. And so it was inevitable that the first islanders were seasonal fishermen.

The biggest island in the Shoals was first called Hog Island because it resembled a hog's back rising from the water. But the smoothly rounded back is deceptive. There is a valley on the island that divides it rather unequally. However, there are many Hog Islands along the northeastern coast, and so, when a homesick Englishman rechristened the island Appledore, the newer name stuck. Appledore, and Smuttynose, its neighbor across the narrow channel, were settled by the 1600s, earlier than most of the mainland.

It was on Appledore that a pre-Revolutionary butcher, Philip Babb, made his home and kept his shop. But Old Babb was more than just a butcher. He was a policeman as well. In 1653 he was made constable of all the Isles of Shoals except for Star Island.

Babb did his duty well, for some years. But then, in the

course of duty Babb learned that pirates had buried treasure on the island. Constable Babb did not turn this interesting information over to the government.* Instead, in the dead of night, with a friend named Ambrose Gibbon to share the work of digging, Babb looked for the gold himself.

They dug a pit near Babb's house, the house that stood on the south hillside above Babb's Cove. The pit was thirty feet across and ten feet deep.

Suddenly Babb's shovel struck metal.

"A chest," he shouted up to Gibbon.

Lantern in hand, Gibbon leaped down into the pit with Babb. Quickly the two men uncovered the chest. It was made of iron and was too heavy to move.

"We'll open her here," said Babb with a growl. "I'll stand guard. Ye get a hammer and chisel."

Mumbling about unequal duties, Gibbon climbed out of the pit and went back to the house for the tools. When he returned, the men worked in silence for about five minutes, trying to lift the treasure chest's lid. The only sound was the hammer striking the cold chisel and the labored breathing of the men. Finally the cover moved just a bit.

"Here she comes," said Babb in a hoarse whisper.

But as they watched, smoke began to pour from the partially opened lid.

Babb and Gibbon, swallowed up in smoke, coughed furiously. The sulphurous smoke burned their lungs, but they kept working on the chest.

---

* *Indeed, some islanders insist that Babb was a member of Captain Kidd's gang of thieves and buried the treasure himself. They say he was then murdered by Kidd for knowing the treasure's location, and left at the site as a ghostly guard. However, since Babb died in 1671 and Kidd was not commissioned a privateer until 1696, it must have been Babb's ghost who joined Kidd's crew!*

With a sudden *snap*, the lid burst open.

"For the love of mercy!" shouted Babb and threw his hands over his head. Gibbon was quicker, and scrambled up the pit's side. Babb was not long after him. As they made it to the top, they glanced back. Red-hot horseshoes were flying out of the chest. The strange missiles pursued them halfway up the beach.

Babb and his friend did not return to the pit that night. In the morning, when they peered over cautiously, the chest was again covered with sand at the bottom of the pit. No one ever saw the treasure chest again. Babb and his friend never dared try to dig it up, and they saw to it that no one else tried during their lifetimes. The great pit remained open until 1851, however, when a storm filled it up.

But according to tradition, the ghost of Old Babb still walks the shingly beach. He wears his coarse, striped, butcher's frock bound round with a leather belt. On the belt is a sheaf that contains a ghostly knife which he brandishes in the face of anyone who dares attempt to find the treasure.

The famous author Nathaniel Hawthorne went so far as to describe Babb as having "a ring around his neck and is supposed either to have been hung or have had his throat cut. . . . There is a luminous appearance about him as he walks, and his face is pale and very dreadful."

Hawthorne himself did not meet the ghost of Babb. But he heard of one man who did. The shoaler was coming around the corner of his workshop when he saw a large man dressed in the coarse, striped, butcher's apron.

Thinking it was a friend playing a joke, the shoaler hailed the costumed figure. At that, it turned around and with ghastly face and hollow eyes, lifted its knife and screamed.

The shoaler did not take time to figure out what Babb's ghost was screaming, but fled to the house of a friend. There he found the man he thought was playing the joke quietly eating his dinner. Of the ghost there was no sight.

Another shoaler saw Philip Babb's spectre on a calm and mild spring evening, just at sunset. As he walked along the beach towards Babb's Cove, he saw a figure approaching him. As the man grew nearer, he recognized the striped frock and belt. He advanced slowly, calling out, "Who are you? What do you want?" But the ghost grew cloudy and slowly dissolved while he watched.

Old Babb's ghost haunted Appledore for almost three centuries. But in the early 1900s the coast guard built a boathouse over the site of the treasure. Since that time, the ghost has not walked. Apparently Philip Babb's shade is at rest, as no one can dig for the chest now. His ghost has not been seen in more than sixty-five years.

Chapter 5

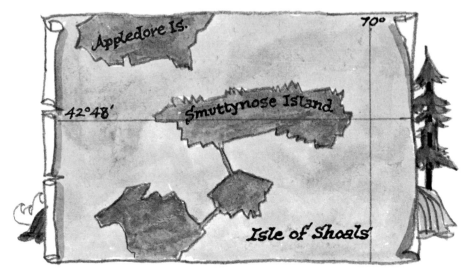

SMUTTYNOSE ISLAND
Latitude: 42°48′ N
Longitude: 70°36′ W

The Ghost of Blackbeard's Wife

Across a narrow channel from Appledore and connected with Cedar by a breakwater, lies a small island with a smutch of dark seaweed on its extended nose. Smuttynose it was called even before it was settled in the 1600s, and Smuttynose it has remained. The black point projecting into the sea contrasts sharply with the pale gneiss, the rocks of which the rest of the Isles of Shoals are formed.

Today the long, low island is privately owned and only one cottage exists on its rocky shores. Perhaps it is just as well, for the island is ghost-ridden. Not only are the shades of shipwrecked Spanish sailors still trying to beg passage home from any passing ship, but the ghost of Blackbeard's fourteenth wife still walks the island's sands.

Edward Teach—Blackbeard he was called by his enemies, and he had many of those—was one of the bloodiest pirates ever to sail the sea. He stole and he murdered, and he enjoyed every minute of his horrid career. To frighten people he would sometimes put phosphorescent fuses in his long, tangled, black beard and light them, looking like a devil just burst out of the flaming underworld, laughing fiendishly while the fuses sputtered and sparkled in his hair. He liked his men terrified and drunk so that he could keep order on his ship. And he was not above killing one of his own men to teach the rest a lesson.

After a long career, Teach managed to buy a pardon in 1718 from Governor Eden of North Carolina. In celebration, Blackbeard sailed off to the Isles of Shoals with his fourteenth wife. His horrible reputation and horrifying manners did not seem to stop women from falling in love with him. It was even said that he was married to all fourteen at once and that the others all lived on Ocracoke Island, off the Carolina coast.

The fourteenth wife was a lovely, gentle, blonde-haired, Scottish girl. Blackbeard had met her in the South when he announced his plans to "retire." After he had successfully bribed the Court of the Vice Admiralty and obtained a pardon for his past sins, Teach proposed to his Scottish-born love.

No one knows for sure if she knew that Teach was already a much married man. Perhaps she did and did not care. The gently-bred girl followed her supposedly reformed husband on board his ship, and they sailed away to the Isles of Shoals in New Hampshire for a very unusual honeymoon.

Teach and his bride spent several weeks burying silver bars and coins on the islands of Londoner and Smuttynose. Just as the last of the coins and the final silver bar was covered over, the lookout spotted a British ship.

"A man-o-war bearing for Londoner Island," called the man.

Teach's sailors ran for their ship. They had violated their

pardons by hiding more treasure. To be caught by the British Navy would mean death—hanging on the yard-arm.

"Wait, I cannot run so fast," cried the fourteenth Mrs. Teach. She had picked up her long skirts and had run as fast as she was able, but she was soon outdistanced by the men.

Blackbeard signaled his men ahead. He turned back towards his bride. "I don't want you to come with us. You are in no danger here. But you would be in danger on the ship. Stay here and guard the treasure. Do not fear. I will return for it," he said. "And for you," he added, almost as an afterthought. Then he kissed his bride and ran for the dinghy where his men were waiting.

Blackbeard the Pirate

The girl was left behind. As she watched, the pirate ship disappeared beyond the horizon, the British ship in full sail right behind.

Teach never was able to return for his wife or his treasure. The Virginia and Carolina planters had organized against him and sent the ship, the *H. M. S. Pearl* out to take him dead or alive. He was caught on November 21 of that year not far from Ocracoke where his thirteen other wives lived. Though he fought desperately with both sword and pistol, Blackbeard died with twenty-five wounds in his body. His head was taken back to the Governor of Virginia on a pole.

His fair young widow wandered the sands of Smuttynose for seventeen lonely years until her own death in 1735.

The islanders say she wanders there still, waiting for Teach's return. During the long years, she has appeared on many of the Isles of Shoals, "fair as a lily and as still" read one newspaper account of her ghost. Wrapped in a long, dark seacloak, her pale hair spilling down over her shoulders, she stands with her face towards the far horizon. Witnesses report that she whispers over and over, "He will come again. He will come again."

But he never comes.

And if you doubt the story, then you should know that in 1820, Captain Samuel Haley, who owned and lived on Smuttynose, was building a wall. He turned over a large flat stone and discovered four bars of solid silver. With the money he built the seawall which connects Smuttynose with Malaga. "Haley's Breakwater" it is called. Or call it proof, if you need help in believing this tale. The rest of Blackbeard's treasure, however, is still buried. Only his widow's ghost knows where it can be found.

Chapter 6

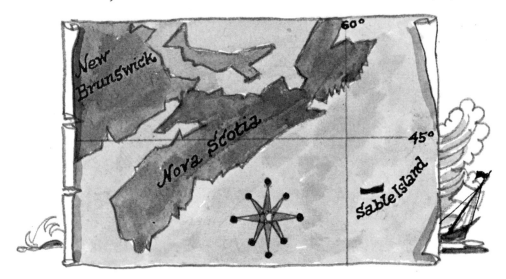

SABLE ISLAND
Latitude: 43° 51′ N
Longitude: 59° 48′ W

The Four-Ghost Island

Ninety miles from Nova Scotia lies a wreck-strewn sand-bar called "the graveyard of the North Atlantic"—Sable Island. On its reefs and beaches, an estimated ten thousand lives and 506 craft have been lost.

Sable Island is known for its chameleon sands, sands that blend in color with the surrounding ocean. It is known for its cranberry bushes that flourish where nothing else will grow. It is known for its herd of shaggy, wild ponies with manes some three feet long. But mostly, Sable Island is known for its wrecks, for the spars of lost ships can still be seen on its shifting sands.

The island itself is continually changing, moving east-ward with each passing year. It is constantly washed away on the west side while it fills in on the east. So it is moving eastward at a rate of one-eighth of a mile per year. Since 1766, it has moved almost twenty-three miles further out to sea from Halifax.

Each shipwreck is a singular tale. Sable Islanders tell many sad stories of lives lost; but they also tell many intriguing tales of bells that toll beneath the waves, and ghosts that walk on the chameleon sands. When the winds howl around the crescent-shaped island and the sands vibrate from end to end with the thunder of the surf, one of the island's four ghosts usually walks.

The oldest of these ghosts is a sixteenth-century Parisian gentleman. He had married a French lady who was as virtuous as she was beautiful. That combination was to be her downfall. When she resisted the advances of Henry IV, the King of France, choosing to remain faithful to her beloved husband, she was sent to prison for treason.

At that same time, 1598, a certain Count de la Roche was planning to start a settlement on Sable Island. Sable was well known by French and Portuguese sailors. Cattle were already on the island, grazing on the sparse scrub grass. They had been left there by the last members of an earlier colony that had failed.

As was the usual procedure, Count de la Roche chose his settlers for the new colony from the French prisons. Colonization was very hazardous in those days. Only prisoners, the poor, or the persecuted—people who saw no other way to better their lot—would "volunteer" to settle a land.

Count de la Roche spent many months scouring the French jails from Brittany to Normandy. He selected nearly a hundred of the worst felons—both men and women—to help found his new colony. Forty of those chosen were lucky. They had enough influence or money to buy their way out. But the Count sailed with the rest.

The Count also had one special prisoner, chosen by the King himself—the lovely but unwilling Parisian lady.

When the ship and its convict crew reached the barren sands of Sable, Count de la Roche changed his mind about staying there himself. Sable looked much too harsh and unwelcoming to him. So he landed the prisoners, including the Parisian lady, left them a few supplies, and sailed back to France's warm weather and fine wines.

But his welcome in France was not what the Count had expected. His creditors seized him and had him imprisoned. If he had made any promises to the island convicts about returning for them in the spring, they were promises he certainly could not keep.

Meanwhile, on the island, the convicts began to quarrel. They quarreled over food. They quarreled over places to sleep. They even quarreled over the few women. A terrible fight broke out that lasted for days. When it was over, many of the convicts were dead, and those who were alive were terribly weakened.

The women convinced them then that the situation was desperate. It was either unite—or die.

So the convicts united. And one week later, as if to reward them for their new-found peace, a Spanish merchant

ship was wrecked on the island. The convicts salvaged food, clothing, seed, farming implements, and a few sheep. The following spring they were even able to till a small sheltered valley. (It is still called "French Gardens.")

But the seasons on Sable Island were too harsh for the poorly supplied convicts. Though the temperature never fell below six degrees, and the men had learned how to catch seals and make clothing out of the skins, the women were too weak to live through the long, cold, barren winters. Five years later, in 1608, when the King of France finally sent a ship for their rescue, there were only eleven men left alive. All the women were dead, including the beautiful Parisian lady.

The eleven remaining convicts were brought back to France and were exhibited to the king in their sealskin clothing. King Henry, aging and much mellowed, was so moved by their story that he gave them a full pardon and fifty gold crowns apiece. French society invited the men to parties. They were the celebrities of the year. But the islanders were unused to society's artificialities. They became uncomfortable and unhappy. They begged to be returned to their island. There, with fresh supplies, they spent the remainder of their lives in relative security as fur trappers, sealers, and ivory traders.

The husband of the beautiful prisoner had been dead five years when the Sable Islanders returned to France. When his beloved wife had been shipped to the New World, he had died of a broken heart. However, his ghost sailed back with the pardoned prisoners when they returned to Sable's shores. And whenever a French vessel comes to (or is wrecked on) Sable Island—even to this day —he appears with his plumed hat in his hand. He seeks out his countrymen and complains, in archaic French, of his treatment by the King. But of course it is centuries too late for anything to be done.

The second ghost of Sable Island is that of an Englishman, one of the Regicides who condemned Charles I to death. This unnamed gentleman, a supporter of Oliver Cromwell, was one of the judges who had ruled that the English king deserved to die because of his misuse of power. And so, in 1649, Charles I lost his head on the axeman's block.

But Charles' sons waited on the continent until Cromwell's death. Then they gathered their loyal forces and returned to England's green shores. Their armies were victorious, and a new king was restored to the throne— King Charles II.

When the Restoration Period began in 1660, everyone who had had anything to do with the old king's death fled. Charles II had sworn vengeance on the men who had killed his father.

Some of the judges, the Regicides, fled to America. This one escaped to Sable Island where he lived quietly for twenty years, and died safely in his own bed.

But every May 29, on the Anniversary of Charles II's return, the ghost of the Regicide marches up and down in noisy protest on Sable's shifting sands. He can be identified by his broad-brimmed hat and his plain Puritan clothes. And he sings psalms so loudly through his nose that he can be heard above the wailing of the wind.

The third Sable Island ghost is a woman. Though her name was Mrs. Copeland when she was alive, dead she is known as The Lady with the Missing Finger. This is her story.

One of the hundreds of vessels wrecked on Sable's shores was a passenger ship from England, the *Princess Amelia*. She was carrying furniture, supplies, and two hundred settlers to Nova Scotia. When she went down, all hands were drowned except Mrs. Copeland.

Though the winds were screaming around her and the waves threatened to rip the hatch cover from her hand, Mrs. Copeland held on to the piece of wood and managed to reach shore at the storm's end.

But this was the eighteenth century. Sable Island was no longer a base for the seal trappers and ivory traders. It was the home of a group of notorious "wreckers." These were men and women who did not just seek out the legitimate salvage from ships wrecked in storms. Often these wreckers would set up false lights to lure ships onto the island. They were pirates who never left the shore. Instead they brought their victims onto the shifting sands of their island.

When the *Princess Amelia*'s wreckage washed ashore, the plunderers were jubilant. They quickly "rescued" the furniture and supplies from the water. They stripped the still-warm corpses of their jewels and clothing.

But then one of the wreckers sighted Mrs. Copeland lying motionless in a shallow pool. She was still clutching the hatch cover. Thinking she was dead, the wrecker went over to her. But as he came closer, he saw that she was breathing, though with difficulty. She was unconscious, but alive. She was so beautiful, that the man's first thought was that he would like to bring her home and have her as his woman. But then he noticed a magnificent emerald ring upon her left hand. Greed overcame lust. He bent down not to help her up but to pull the ring from her finger. However, she had been in the water so long that her fingers were swollen. The ring would not come off.

When she felt someone pulling at her hand, Mrs. Copeland began to regain consciousness. Instinctively, she pulled back.

When Mrs. Copeland started to struggle, the wrecker put his hands around her throat. At first he meant just to silence her, stop her struggles until he could get the ring.

But the poor woman was so weak from the cold hours in the sea, that she died almost immediately. When the wrecker saw this, he calmly cut off the finger with the ring and put ring and finger into his pocket.

When he got home that evening, the wrecker brought the grisly prize from his pocket to show his wife. She screamed and ran out of the house. It was only then that he began to realize the horror of what he had done. Soon after this, he sold his house and his part of the wrecking business, and moved to Cape Breton to find a new and better way of life. But bad luck had followed him ever since that evil night, and at last he had to pawn whatever he could. The emerald ring brought only twenty shillings.

In 1803, Prince Edward, the Governor of Nova Scotia, finally decided to act against the many wreckers who were luring ships onto the rocks and sands of Nova Scotia and the coastal islands. He sent his most trustworthy captain, Edmund Torrens, to Sable to arrest the Sable wreckers. Torrens sailed out in the brig *Harriot*. As luck would have it, they met a fierce storm. The *Harriot* was dashed onto the chameleon sands of Sable and all but six men and a dog were drowned.

Quickly the remaining men under Torrens buried their dead. They built a shelter and set a guard until they could be rescued. The wreckers, seeing that it was a government ship, had left them alone.

Torrens decided to check their surroundings. He took the dog and began to walk down the long beach eastward towards land's end. Several hours later, when the sun began to go down, he realized he was too far away to return that night. So he turned inland. Soon he spied a small building.

As Captain Torrens neared the building, the dog began to growl. Torrens reached down to calm the animal and found it was shaking. It was not a dog on alert, it was a very frightened animal. The dog began to whimper and refused to go into the shelter. Torrens ignored the animal, and gathered hay and firewood for a bed.

Still the dog cowered outside. So before dark had entirely set in, in an attempt to calm the dog, Torrens went for a walk with the animal near a lovely saltwater lake.

They returned in the dark. No sooner did they reach the shelter then the dog began to bark frantically. Torrens took a warning from the dog, and entered the shelter with his pistol cocked.

Inside the hut, outlined by the hearthfire, sat a stately woman drying her long dark hair. Her floor-length gown was torn and stained. And when she looked up, the Captain could see that tears glistened in her eyes.

"Who are you, Madame?" he whispered.

The woman did not answer. Instead, she held up her left hand. Torrens could see that a finger was missing. Blood dripped from her hand.

Quickly Torrens moved towards her to help her. "May I bandage it for you?" he asked.

The woman jumped up as if in fear, and pushed past him out into the night. By the time Torrens recovered himself, she had disappeared.

The next morning the Captain made his way back to his small crew. He was convinced that the woman was mad. But she was also obviously in great pain, and he knew he would have to find her again. Leaving the dog with the others for fear it would frighten the woman away, Torrens went back to the hut.

When he entered, the woman was there again. The embers of the fire still smouldered. This time Captain Torrens managed to get closer to the lady. She lifted up her ravaged face and the Captain stared in shock.

"Mrs. Copeland," he gasped. He recognized her. She was the beautiful wife of the Seventh Regiment's surgeon.

He moved closer and as he did, her outline began to waver in the firelight. Then he remembered the story of the wreck of the *Princess Amelia* and how the surgeon's wife had never returned from her trip. Suddenly Captain Torrens understood.

"You were murdered," he whispered.

The ghost nodded.

"I swear I will find the man," Torrens said.

The ghost shook her head and held up her hand.

"You only want what is yours?" he guessed aloud.

The ghost managed a slow smile.

"A ring?"

She nodded, then slipped past him out the door. She was gone before he got outside.

The Captain went back to his sailors, but he did not tell any of them what had occurred. Several days later they were rescued by a government ship. While the others put their Sable Island misadventure behind them, Captain Torrens could not. He kept thinking about the suffering etched into that ghostly face and how he had promised he would find the ring.

Because Torrens was Prince Edward's man, he was able to extract information where others might have failed. In time, he learned the identity of the suspected wrecker who had escaped the island. Torrens found out about the man's Cape Breton home. He journeyed there in disguise, as a merchant, wearing on his hand a cheap, gaudy ring with a bright green stone.

When Torrens arrived, the man of the house was not there. He had gone to Labrador to find work. But passing himself off as an old friend, the Captain had dinner with the family.

The youngest daughter noticed his ring as they sat at the table.

"Why Maman," she exclaimed, "that's just like the ring Papa showed us. Don't you remember?"

At those words, Maman had gone white. She explained hastily to their guest that it was a ring her husband had gotten from a Frenchman who had found the ring in the Sable sands. "Probably from a wreck," she added.

Torrens nodded pleasantly, though he knew too well what shipwreck it was from.

"I would love to see this ring," he said. "I collect rings, and I could tell you if it is of value."

"Oh, it was sold in Halifax some months ago," came the reply.

Captain Torrens made a rather hasty but polite farewell after dinner and hurried to Halifax.

Luck was with the gallant Captain, for there were at

that time only two watchmaker-pawn shops in all of Halifax. He located the ring and made a special trip back to Sable Island. He left the ring before the fireplace in the tiny hut. When he returned the next day, the ring was gone.

But it seems the ghost was not satisfied. For she still walks along the Sable sands. And those who have seen her say she waves her left hand when anyone approaches. A left hand with only four fingers.

The last Sable Island ghost was once a native-born resident of the island.

When Prince Edward cleared the island of the wreckers in 1804, he established a government station there. (The complex today consists of two lighthouses, a lifesaving station, a wireless station, and a weather station, all manned by officials and their families.)

The overriding duty of all the people who lived at the government station on Sable was to save and protect ships from the terrible island sands. Yet in the less than two hundred years since the establishment of the government

facilities, still more than two hundred vessels have been lost.

In 1856, in one terrible storm, one of the island men on his way to help salvage a wrecked ship fell out of the lifeboat and was drowned. His body was never found.

But the next year, when the lifeboat put out to shore on yet another rescue attempt, the rescuers were shorthanded. So they left the bowseat empty.

The Sable men rowed as hard as they could towards the foundering ship. Just as they passed the middle bar, one of the younger men gave a startled cry. "Look!" he called and the men turned towards his pointing finger.

A ghostly hand reached out of the roiling sea. But no water seemed to drip from it. It grabbed hold of the side of the boat. Suddenly with a heave, a ghostly figure pulled itself in. It took the unclaimed oar and began to row. The ghostly lifesaver rowed evenly and calmly as though well used to the task.

The lifeboat reached the sinking ship in time. They managed to reach a number of survivors and placed them carefully in the boat. Then the men pulled oars for home.

Just as they came to the middle bar, the ghostly lifesaver dove over the gunwale into the water.

For many years after, the rescuers left the bowseat empty for their ghostly helper. And for many years—until the advent of more modern rescue operations—he came to help.

Sable Island lies on the shipping lanes between North America and Europe. As long as those shipping lanes are used, the half-moon island will lie in wait like some hungry beast, ready to pounce on its unsuspecting prey. And as long as the dune sands lie shifting, changing under the water, the ghosts of Sable will walk along the island's shore.

Mystery Islands

Mystery Islands

Just as an island is the perfect place for a ghost to walk, so too it is the perfect place for a mystery. The isolation of an island, cut off from mainland influences and mainland eyes, is just the right setting for a puzzle.

These next three stories are cosmic puzzles; not just simple mysteries, but mysteries on such a large scale that scientific detectives as well as novelists, clairvoyants, archaeologists, seismologists, anthropologists, biologists, explorers, and pirates have been trying to solve them for centuries.

In each case, the mystery is not only what is on the island and who is on the island, or what was on the island and who was on the island, but also much of the mystery is due to the island itself.

It is interesting that the word mystery comes from the Latin mysterium and the Greek mysterion meaning "the secret worship of a secret thing." It is also interesting to know that it was a medieval convention to call the site of anything that was full of marvels an "island." Think of these old meanings when you read the mysteries of the next three islands.

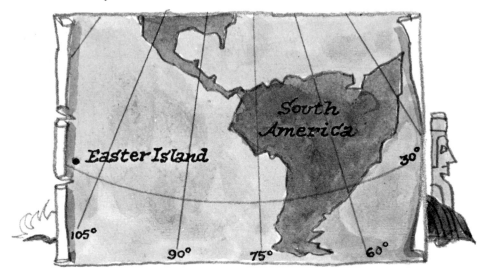

Chapter 7

EASTER ISLAND
Latitude: 27° S
Longitude: 109° W

The Great Stone Mystery

It was on Easter Day in 1722 that Dutch captain Jacob Roggeveen sailed his three small ships to an island 2350 miles from the coast of South America. That lonely piece of land was 1400 miles from the nearest inhabited island, and Roggeveen was guided to it by smoke that curled up over the island.

Roggeveen sighted the smoke on Easter Day and so he named the island in honor of that day—Paasch Eyland, Easter Island. At sunset he ordered the anchors dropped and stared across at the rugged grey-green hills and the cliffs that sheared off into the sea.

Captain Roggeveen was puzzled. Something strange and awesome was on that island. As he stared, the shapes that seemed to repeat themselves all over the island became more clearly visible to him. It looked as though great crowned giants were standing and staring back. But the giants never moved, though Roggeveen watched for many minutes. He realized at last that they must be statues. But the size of them! Why for him to see them from his ship they must be at least as tall as a house! Their crowns alone must weigh as much as elephants.

But Captain Roggeveen had little time for more speculation. The first of the native population had come out on boats to greet the Dutchmen.

The first greeters were mostly tall, rather fair-skinned Polynesian men, not unlike Hawaiians or Tahitians. One, Roggeveen later described as "a completely white man." His ceremonious air made the sailors believe he was a priest. He had a crown of feathers on his close-shaven head, and in his ears were white pegs as big as fists. The pegs had lengthened his earlobes so that they fell down to his shoulders. There were many islanders with ears that long. But not all the natives were fair-skinned. Among the men who came aboard to greet them were also some small, darker men.

Before it completely turned night, the natives returned to their island. In the morning, a hundred watchfires were burning on the island, making the smoke that Roggeveen had first sighted. As the sailors watched from their ship, the natives stretched themselves before the fires and worshipped the rising sun.

When the Dutchmen went ashore, they made a careful inspection of the giant statues. These proved to be well over thirty feet high. Many wore red topknots or hats, like a kind of crown. They were crudely but powerfully carved statues of long-eared Polynesians, and so heavy that it seemed impossible that they had been lifted onto their stone bases without the use of machines. Yet the islanders were still living as if in the Stone Age. They had

no machines at all. To make matters more mysterious, the islanders seemed to have no ropes in their possession, nor were there many trees on the island from which levers to raise the giant statues could have been made.

It was such a puzzle that the Dutchmen explained it away as best they could. They decided that the statues must not be made of stone at all, but rather modeled in clay and afterwards—to make them heavy—stuffed with small stones.

Though their visit started out in a friendly manner, some sort of argument or misunderstanding arose between the Dutchmen and the islanders. When the Dutchmen killed several islanders, and wounded some others, they hastily concluded their stay.

And for nearly fifty years the island and its statues were left in peace.

In 1770, another expedition landed on the island. This time the sailors were Spaniards, and they, too, were attracted by the smoke signals. They landed with great ceremony, forming a parade that consisted of two priests, a large contingent of soldiers, and cheering natives. They marched to the top of three small hills, planted a Spanish flag on each hill, and declared the island be called *San Carlos*, the property of King Charles of Spain.*

Of course the mysterious stone statues intrigued them, too. After striking a statue with an iron hoe that caused sparks to fly, the Spaniards—unlike the Dutch—were convinced that the giants were made of stone. The leader of the Spaniards, Don Felipe Gonzales, concluded that the statues had never been made on the island at all, but that they had been brought from afar. But from where? His question was never answered.

---

* *No one, of course, had asked the natives what they called their island. To them it was known as* Marae-Toe-Hau, *The Burial Place,* and Te-Pito-te-Henua, *The Navel of the Deep.*

Next, in 1774, the intrepid Captain Cook visited the island. After him, in 1786, the French explorer La Perouse spent half a day there. When the English came, a new dimension was added to the mystery, for the ships carried a Polynesian sailor who could understand some of the islanders' dialect. Through the Polynesian, the English learned that the islanders did not regard the statues as images of gods but rather as monuments to early royal personages who had lived on the island. The English also investigated the great walled terraces that stood on the island, terraces that were composed of huge stone blocks so precisely cut and polished that they have stood for centuries without mortar. The English and the French were unable to explain either the statues or the stone walls.

And Easter Island was left alone to the sea and the sky and the silent guidance of the great stone statues until the beginning of the 1800s. Then the Americans came for a visit.

It was the start of slaving on Easter Island. First some men and women were kidnapped by an American schooner captain to be colonists on a sealing station. In years that followed, Peruvian sailors raided the unsuspecting islanders and carried off a number of them to be laborers on the offshore islands of Peru. By 1862, Easter Island was nearly depopulated, for more than a thousand islanders had been carried off to work.

The bishop of Tahiti worked to have the islanders returned, and he was somewhat successful. Unfortunately, by the time the Peruvian government had them returned to Easter Island, there were not many of the erstwhile slaves left. Nine hundred had already died of various illnesses or from their inability to adjust to new and strange living conditions. Of the hundred who started the trip back, nearly all died during the voyage. Only *fifteen* men returned to Easter Island alive. They brought with them a gift from civilization—smallpox. It spread rapidly through the island as the remaining islanders came to greet their returned friends and relatives. Before the year was out, the entire island population fell to a mere hundred and eleven people, including children.

The Easter Islanders had been brutalized and killed by their contact with the world. Then in 1864, they were converted to Christianity by Brother Eugene Eyaud. Slowly they lost touch with their proud ancestors who had raised the statues on the island so many centuries before. For at the same time that Christianity was brought to the island, the natives' *rongo-rongo* tablets were discovered—and destroyed. Carved on these tablets, "the singing wood" as they were called by the islanders, were stories in hieroglyphics. They were stories relating to death and rebirth; probably some contained history and other information. But most of the tablets were destroyed by over-zealous missionaries who thought them objects of pagan ritual. And their secret language—perhaps related to Egyptian picture language or to the Mayan hieroglyphics —has never been deciphered.

\ The mystery of Easter Island began to fascinate more and more people. And the mystery, as the world then saw it, was this: Who originally populated Easter Island? Who built the statues? How did they move the statues —without tools, without trees, without ropes—from wherever they had been sculpted to their lonely outposts on the island's edges. And what did they really stand for?

But the mystery went deeper than that. Who supplied the food for the island's original inhabitants? Easter Island itself did not seem to have the means. Yet there was no shipping trade to bring food to the stone masons while they worked. For if the stone masons were, themselves,

farmers, when did they have time to carve and carry the stones? If they were carving and carrying the statues, when did they have time to grow food?

And there was more to it, even, than that!

In 1955 an expedition, under the leadership of the adventurous archaeologist Thor Heyerdahl, journeyed to Easter Island especially to solve the mystery of the island. But the Norwegian expedition was introduced to still a greater puzzle. These explorers were well received by the islanders and shown many of the heretofore hidden caves of the natives. And they were also shown around the volcanic crater-workshop Rano Raraku where the island's statues had been carved. For despite Don Gonzales' belief that these stones had been brought from elsewhere, the giant statues had been carved from the island's own hills.

When Heyerdahl and his crew were brought to the crater-workshop, they found that the whole mountain had been reshaped by the stone sculptors. There were 150 unfinished statues near the rock faces and on the crater edges. At the foot of the mountain were a line of finished stone men, like an army awaiting a supernatural command. And each stone face wore the same impassive expression; on each head was carved the strange long ears. Later when the crew members dug around these heads, they found there were bodies attached to them, trunks carved down to the hips and distended bellies, with long arms and hands, and fingers with curved nails that met under the protruding stomachs. Over the centuries the sand had slowly sifted around the statues, covering their lower parts until only the heads remained out in the open, exposed to the wind and stars.

There was no doubt that here, in the bowels of Easter Island itself, years before Christopher Columbus had discovered America, ancient stone sculptors with stone adzes

created, in Heyerdahl's words, one of the "greatest en-
gineering projects of all time."

But why were so many statues left uncompleted? Why
were the simple stone tools left lying about, as if as suddenly as they had appeared on Easter Island, the stone
sculptors had disappeared again? It was yet another mystery to add to the others.

The natives spoke of strange birdmen who had flown
to the island, rather than sailing to it on the sea. Some
modern authors, notably Erich von Daniken, have specu-
lated that Easter Island is one of the clues that points to
a pre-historic visit to our planet by beings from some

other world. They speculate that spaceships plowed the oceans of the skies long before sailing ships on Earth's seas reached Easter Island. Certainly the statues bear a startling resemblance to those in some Indian ruins in South America. And certainly all the legends of flying birdmen cannot be totally discounted. Is this theory any stranger than that of the Spaniards, that primitive men had somehow carried tons of rocks across thousands of ocean miles to carve and set them on a lonely island outpost?

Thor Heyerdahl's expedition attempted to answer some of the mysteries. Heyerdahl explained, in his book *Aku-Aku*, how the stone giants had been carved. Each one took six men a year to complete.

The modern natives showed Heyerdahl the method that had been handed down father-to-son for generations. They had been carved slowly with the stone implements, head first and then belly until at last, only a small section of the back was still attached to the crater formed by the carving out of the statue. Then the statues were pulled up to a standing position. Only then was the back finished off.

But how had the men raised statues that size, the largest of which was as high as a seven-story house? Again, the natives showed Heyerdahl and his crew. Their method consisted of shoving three poles under the head of the statue to lift it by fractions of an inch. Then they pushed tiny stones under the statue. As more stones were wedged in, their size increased. After several days, the statue was lifted into the air on an ever-growing tower of stones.*

* *In fact, Captain Cook had suggested this as a possibility back in 1774, and it might have been he who first mentioned it to the natives. He wrote: "The only method I can conceive is by raising the upper end by little and little, supporting it by stones as it is raised, and building about it till they got it erect . . ."*

Next, the over six hundred statues had been moved down the mountainside, without chipping or damaging the polished stone, to settings as far away as ten miles. The smallest of these statues weighed from two to ten tons apiece. How such a move was accomplished has yet to be adequately explained.

After that, the statues were set upon platforms above the ground, holes were chiseled for the eyes, and then the two-elephant-weight crowns were placed on top of the heads. (These red topknots had meanwhile been quarried from a different crater seven miles from Rano Raraku.)

All this sounds difficult, almost impossible. Thor Heyerdahl explained such a feat in modern terms. Suppose, he suggested, we take "a ten-ton boxcar and turn it upside down, for the wheel was unknown in Polynesia. Next we capsize another boxcar alongside the first one, and tie the two firmly together. Then we drive twelve full-grown horses into the cars, and after them five large elephants. Now we have got our fifty tons and can begin to pull. We have not merely to move this weight, but drag it for two and a half miles over stony ground without the slightest injury being done to it. Is this impossible without machinery? If so, the oldest inhabitants of Easter Island mastered the impossible."

Today, the statues—with the aid of modern machinery —are being restored and set up again all over the island. Yet most of the mysteries, the whos, hows, and whys, remain to be solved.

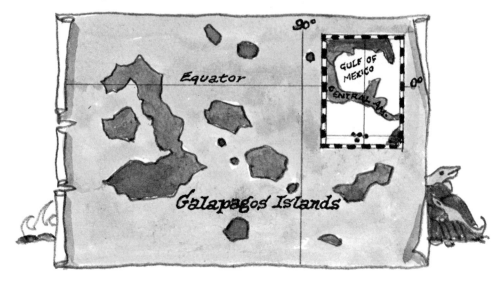

Chapter 8

THE GALAPAGOS
Latitude: 0°
Longitude: 90° W

The Islands Time Forgot

On March 10, 1535, a ship full of Spanish sailors came upon a strange group of islands six hundred miles west of the South American coast. Eagerly they landed, for they were sea-weary and hungry for more than the meager stores aboard their ship.

When they came ashore, they discovered themselves in a world so new that they thought they had been enchanted. In fact, ever after, the islands were nicknamed the *Islas Encantadas*, the Enchanted Isles.

On the islands, the sailors found the strangest animals they had ever seen in all their seafaring lives: tortoises so big that a man could ride atop one, small dragons four feet long, wingless birds that strode on the rocky shores, and tiny finches so tame that they would fly onto a sailor's outstretched hand.

The Spaniards were but the first of a long line of fascinated visitors who charted the Encantadas or, as they were called (after the giant turtles, *galápagos* in Spanish), the Galapagos. Many buccaneers and pirates made the islands their stopping-off place as they escaped from the navy's guns. Sealers and whalers came to get provisions from the ever-green isles. Scientists came to the islands in fascinated groups to study the strange ecology. And writers, equally dazzled by the mysterious archipelago, wrote about the Enchanted Isles in fact and fiction. Each visitor left his mark, not so much on the islands, but on history. For as men learned about the Encantadas, they learned about humankind as well.

What did they learn? And what did they not learn?

The Galapagos Islands could be called a textbook of evolution, a "keyhole into time." It is a place where some mysteries have been solved and still others begun. It helped man learn about his beginnings, helped him watch the process of growth, and pointed out some lessons about the future as well.

The man who first looked through the "keyhole into time" and understood what he saw was a scientist named Charles Darwin. When Darwin was a young man, in 1831, he sailed as the ship's naturalist on the *H. M. S. Beagle* on a five-year voyage of exploration and discovery.

Darwin had been taught, as most people were then, that God had created the world in seven days. Or if not literally in seven days, at least the world had been created all at once by a single creator. But one of the places the *H. M. S. Beagle* stopped at was the Galapagos. The sights, the animals, the strange world that young Darwin saw on his short visit to the Enchanted Isles changed his whole vision of life. He carried his memories of the islands with him for twenty-five years, after which time Darwin published his book *The Origin of Species*. In that book he articulated, for the first time, the thought that man had not just been set down whole on the earth in his present form. Rather, said Darwin, man—and all animals—developed, or *evolved* from other, less complex kinds of animals and organisms. It was the Galapagos that started Darwin along this line of thought for it was those islands which, in his own words, ". . . both in space and time . . . brought [us] somewhat near to that great fact—the mystery of mysteries—the first appearance of new beings on earth."

What was it about the Galapagos animals that made Darwin and other visitors see new things, make new discoveries? It was, as Darwin said, that "the greater number of its inhabitants, both vegetable and animal, [are] found nowhere else."

The *galapagos*, the giant turtles, lumber like great armored tanks all about the islands. They weigh up to five hundred pounds and are thought to live several hundred years. They were called Hecatee, after a medieval witch, by the superstitious pirates who roamed these shores,

because there seemed something magical, ageless, and wise about these enormous beings. All across the islands today one can see smooth paths. They were worn by the turtles, ponderously laboring up and down the rocks, through the vegetation, on their way to and from their waterholes. The giant tortoises crawl at a slow pace—four miles a day. And nothing will stop them, with the exception of a large tree or an equally enormous rock. If the tortoises butt up against some immovable object, they will keep trying to push their way through, for days and weeks at a time, until at last hunger forces them to move a few inches one way or another and go around. Herman Melville, who wrote *Moby Dick*, was fascinated by the Galapagos turtles. He wrote of them that "They seemed newly crawled forth from beneath the foundations of the world." And indeed these elephantine tortoises look as though they have come from another place, another time, so unchanged they are, so un-evolved from their ancestors many thousands of years removed in place and time.

So, too, the four-foot-long iguanas, drowsing on the rocks, seem to be fairy-tale dragons from another time. They have spiny crests from the backs of their heads to the tips of their tails, daggerlike claws, and dangerous-looking sawlike teeth. But they are gentle souls, warning with a hiss, and backing away from any fight. The land iguanas are yellow and red, colors that seem to reflect the color of the surrounding cactus. Fine swimmers, they spend most of the day basking on the black lava rocks, only occasionally wriggling into the water. Once in the water, they join their black brothers of the sea, the marine iguanas, who live on seaweed that grows forty to sixty feet below the water. There are no other iguanas as big as these in all the world.

The turtles and iguanas are the chief inhabitants of the Galapagos. They are so numerous that Melville wrote of the islands: "No voice, no low, no howl is heard; the chief sound of life here is a hiss."

Yet there is another kind of strange life, here: bird life. The Galapagos flightless cormorant is the only cormorant in the world that has completely lost the use of its wings. A clumsy walker but a good swimmer, the cormorant that lives in the Galapagos is also the largest of its kind in the world. Penguins live here, too, which is very strange as the Galapagos are tropical islands. Penguins are ordinarily found only in cold places such as the Arctic and Antarctic.

Stranger still are the finches. The finch is an ordinary little bird, a common type found all over the world. But only in the Galapagos lives a finch that has learned to use a tool to find its food. This finch, which adores the slugs and larvae that hide in cracks and crevices, lacks the woodpecker's drill-like beak. So to compensate, the Galapagos finch breaks off a twig or a cactus spine and,

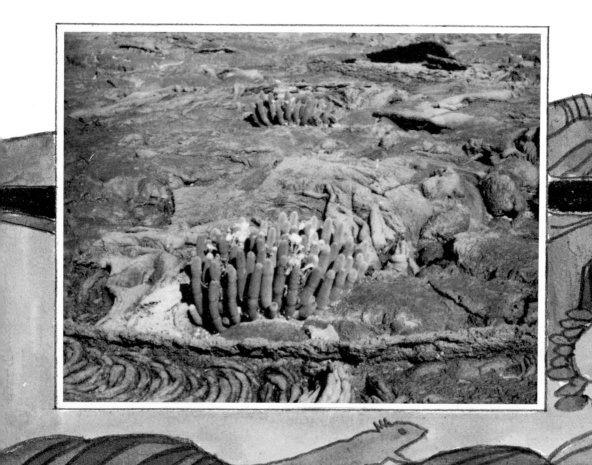

holding it in its beak, uses the tool to dig out the grubs and larvae. Then the finch snaps at its food, dropping the tool in the process, and has lunch. Another slug, another tool.

On another of the islets in the archipelago, the finches do not use this twig-tool, but have developed stronger beaks. In fact, the finches vary from island to island in the island chain. It was this startling discovery, more than any other, that started young Charles Darwin thinking about the possibility of evolution. It seemed obvious to him that pairs of finches had originally flown from the coast some six hundred and fifty miles away. But once on the islands, they had settled down and stayed, each pair or group on a separate island. And each island's finches developed differently for their different needs.

What Darwin saw on the Galapagos was that these volcanic islands were relatively newly created. The islands

were summits of huge volcanoes that rose as much as ten thousand feet from the ocean floor. Each of the islands was a paradise for the animals on it. There was little competition for food, no large predators or natural enemies, a warm and fairly fertile, tropical land, and they were isolated from man's interference, too. The isolation was important, Darwin knew, to the strange ecology of the islands. The results of that isolation showed in the different strains of animals that had developed: 89% of the reptiles, 75% of the birds, 47% of the plants, and 37% of the offshore fish were *absolutely* unique to this archipelago. Even ordinary goats and pigs that the buccaneers had left were so changed as to be different animals. Here, in less than three hundred years, goats as big as ponies had developed; feral pigs that feasted on cactus and the eggs of ground-nesting birds ran wild.

What did this mean? It was a question that Darwin asked himself over and over.

One of the answers he found to that question was that there had to be some ongoing creative force at work, a force he called *evolution*. The idea that God had made these islands in seven days at the same time He had made the rest of the world, in the words of an anonymous reviewer in 1831, could "scarcely fall within the sphere of credibility."

Most of the scientific world has come to accept Darwin's theory of evolution. But the many mysteries of the Galapagos are by no means all solved. We still do not know how the reptiles and birds all got to the islands. We do not know why they stayed. We do not understand exactly how and why things changed there as they did.

There are almost three thousand people living on the islands today, many of them scientists working in the great natural laboratory that is the archipelago. For them the mysteries of the Galapagos are continuing challenges, the islands full of natural marvels.

Chapter 9

ATLANTIS
Latitude: ???
Longitude: ???

The Lost Civilization

Once upon a time, about nine thousand years ago, there was a great island empire called Atlantis. It was located, wrote the Greek philosopher Plato in two stories called *Timaeus* and *Critias*, to the west beyond the Pillars of Hercules.

Atlantis was a green and fertile island civilization consisting of one Great Island, one Round Island, and scattered outposts. All together they made up a great maritime empire. Established by the god Poseidon, Atlantis contained the most technically advanced and cultured people in the ancient world. They were literate, built beautiful roads and canals, laid out gardens and groves inside and outside their palaces, fashioned villas in which modern plumbing existed, and were devoted to such sports as horse racing and hunting bulls. Trade was the cornerstone of their empire's wealth, yet the Atlanteans also backed their trade with an army of one million soldiers and a fleet of twelve thousand vessels.

Sad to say, the islanders grew lazy and, at length corrupt. The sea god, Poseidon, decided he had to destroy his people. So he sent fire and water to devour them.

In a single day and night, the entire island empire of Atlantis vanished. As Plato said, it "disappeared in the depths of the sea."

Since that time, according to Plato, Atlantis had not been seen again.

But from Plato's time to ours, it has been heard of—again and again. The mystery of Atlantis is probably the most popular one in the world. Over two thousand books and articles have been written about the Lost Continent, the Antediluvian World, the Insular Eden since Plato first mentioned it in 355 B.C. Some of the books and articles have been straight fiction, some have been fiction masquerading as fact, and some fact mixed with fiction.

That is the problem with the story of Atlantis. No one knows if it is totally true. Or if it is partially true. Or if there is no truth to the story at all. Ever since Plato first detailed the story of Atlantis' civilization, the argument has been going on.

Plato's own student Aristotle said of the Atlantis story that: "The man who dreamed it up made it vanish." He dismissed the island empire as simply a thing of Plato's dreams. Many critics since, including the famous nineteenth-century scholar Benjamin Jowett, agree. Said Jowett: "the world, like a child, has readily, and for the most part unhesitatingly, accepted the tale." Less sceptical readers see in Plato's tale a strong satire on the Athenian politics of his day. Encyclopedias list Atlantis as "a large *mythical* island in the Atlantic."

Yet for twenty-three centuries, songs and tales and legends about Atlantis have attracted people all over the world. People have sought the "mythical" island from North Africa to Ceylon, from the Azores to the South Pole. Is it because we want so much to believe in a beautiful lost civilization? Or is it that there is a basic truth in the legend that is trying to find its way out?

Crantor, who in 300 B.C. was the first editor of *Timaeus*, thought the story true in every part. He even sent a special inquiry to Egypt, from which country Plato claimed the Atlantis story had originated.

In the sixteenth century, Sir Francis Bacon was sure that America was the Atlantis which had been lost to the sea.

In the seventeenth century, Olof Rudbeck said Atlantis was really part of Sweden. His followers believed that the lemmings who set off to sea from Sweden's shores were searching for a land which had been submerged.

The nineteenth-century American antiquarian, Ignatius Donnelly, wrote volumes on the subject of *Atlantis: The Antediluvian World* and eventually made Atlantism into a popular mystical cult. In fact Donnelly, in a pseudo-scientific manner, "proved" that both the Mayan and Phoenician civilizations were offshoots of Atlantis. And furthermore "proved" that all Europe, America, and Asia had been started as Atlantean colonies.

In between the critics who say that Atlantis is only a pleasant story and the believers who accept the story entirely as true are the people who feel that the tale of Atlantis—like other myths—may embody a hard core of historical fact. These people say that Atlantis is a real tradition embroidered upon by generations of storytellers. And they further feel that what Plato set down was a distorted version of an Egyptian tale about what once had been a real island civilization.

If this is so, what was the true story? Where was the real civilization?

An exciting recent discovery that links Atlantis with a real island empire has been made in an area near Greece itself.

On the island of Crete, in the Aegean Sea, some sixty miles from the Greek mainland, was a flourishing civilization sixteen hundred years before the birth of Christ. Called Minoan after its most powerful ruler King Minos, the civilization spread its tentacles of power to the neighboring island of Thera and to scattered outposts in the Aegean Sea.

In 1895, Sir Arthur Evans began excavating on the island of Crete, at the great palace of Knossos. It was then that the Minoan civilization was rediscovered. It was proved that Crete had been a federation of island cities under King Minos' rule. One of the most fascinating aspects of the Minoan empire had been its worship of bulls. Bull-dancing was a palace sport where young girls and boys—usually of noble birth—performed acrobatics over the horns of a charging bull. Again and again, the bull

motif was found in artwork on the palace walls and pottery, even on jewelry found at the excavation sites. As scholars knew so well, the bull was sacred to the sea god, Poseidon. It was clear that the people who lived on Crete during the Minoan civilization, worshipped the god of the sea.

Another unusual aspect of the Minoan civilization was its sophisticated system of roads, palace buildings, and bathing rooms inside the villas.

Around 1500 B.C., this great maritime power suddenly ceased to be. The palace and villas on Crete were consumed by some kind of great natural cataclysm. The archaeological evidence pointed to a combination of fire and water. Sir Arthur Evans and his diggers had no explanation for the disaster.

In 1909, it was argued in a British newspaper by Professor K. T. Frost that Crete and its neighboring island of Thera might possibly be related to the Atlantis story. But no one paid any attention.

Then in 1939, a Greek archaeologist began to excavate on Thera. Spyridon Marinatos began digging on the small Aegean island and his discoveries proved that once Thera and its smaller neighbor Aspronisi had been a single *round* island. In fact the single island had been known as Stronghyle, or "Round Island." This old Round Island had been a scant sixty miles from the great island of Crete. But crescent-shaped Thera had been torn from Aspronisi around 1500 B.C. by such strong volcanic convulsions that the islands were still layered with more than two inches of volcanic dust. An area some 150 miles by 300 miles had been covered with the white volcanic ash, blanketing most of Crete and the entire Aegean. Waves as big as walls had been pushed onto islands and shores for miles around. This looked, indeed, like the great cataclysm for which Evans and his diggers had been looking.

Yet peculiarly enough, even with this evidence that there had once been a Great Island and a Round Island that had been partially destroyed by fire and water in a great disaster well before Plato's story, no one connected them with Atlantis.

Then at last, in 1967, when at the site of Thera's modern city of Akrotiri an ancient Minoan city was discovered, many archaeologists began to put two and two together. At the site of the ancient city, whose destruction was carbon dated at 1450 B.C., were found two- and three-story buildings with brilliant-colored painted frescoes. One in particular was a red, blue, and gold-ocher depiction of two swallows kissing in mid-air above a field of nodding red lilies. In the buildings themselves were found such artifacts of a sophisticated civilization as jars of wine and oil—with the contents preserved—weaving looms, bronze pots and pans, pottery with classic Minoan designs, and storage vessels large enough to hold a man. There were skeletons of domestic animals but so few human remains that it suggested the thirty thousand people of the city had had prior warning of the coming disaster and had fled.

Evidently the volcano on Thera had begun to erupt sporadically about 1500 B.C. There were several different layers of the volcanic ash. Each time, rebuilding was done on the same sites. The eruptions proceeded by stages to a grand climax some fifty years later when the volcano spit out enough fire and rocks to engulf hundreds of square miles of the Aegean. The skies turned black with the smoke. Huge waves pushed up on the shores, gobbling houses, villas, and palaces alike. Only the palace of Knossos which was well inland was spared to some extent. But the Minoan civilization, that great sea empire built on the two islands, was devastated. The remnants were raided by pirates and finally the neighboring Greeks took over the palace. And by the time Plato was writing, some one thousand years later, almost all *real* memory of the Minoans had been wiped out.

But traces were left. Half-heard stories about the bull-dancers, the bull-worshippers, the large palace at Knossos, the people of Poseidon survived. Remains of the Knossos baths and the great roads could still be seen. And the stories of the big fire, the blackened skies, the huge waves were passed down from father to son, mother to daughter; the tales of the day and night the island had sunk into the sea.

If all this is true—and there are many scientists and archaeologists today who believe it—then Thera and Crete combined *are* Atlantis. Even if it is half true, there is a good possibility that Plato, like any fine storyteller, took what he wanted from real life and used it for his own purposes.

Atlantis remains the most romantic and beautiful of the island mysteries, with its suggestion of a great lost civilization. Perhaps at last we are coming closer to solving this intriguing puzzle.

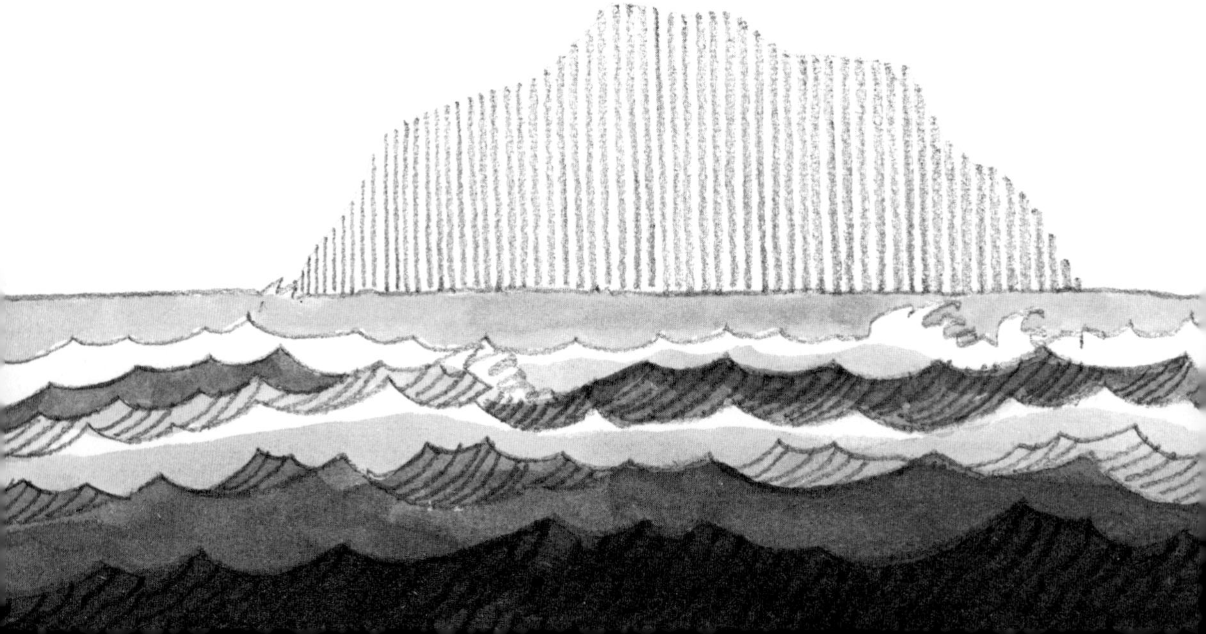

Disappearing Islands

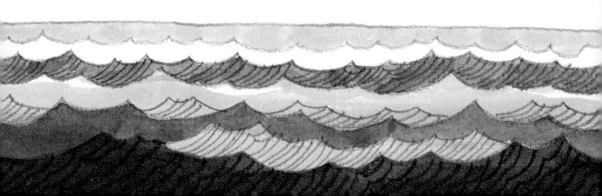

Disappearing Islands

The charts of the world's waters are sprinkled with black dots of islands like pepper grains on a blue tablecloth. Some of the grains are marked E.D., existence doubtful. Some are marked P.D., position doubtful.

These are islands which have been sighted once or twice and never seen again; or islands that appear suddenly in a part of the ocean over which hundreds of ships have already sailed. These are islands that appear in the spyglass of one captain and not in the binoculars of another.

This does not mean that the captains of long ago who charted some of these islands necessarily had faulty vision or faulty instruments. Nor were their latitudinal or longitudinal readings necessarily incorrect, though in poet Walter de la Mare's words, "any map is romance in shorthand." Many of the E.D. islands that were sighted in the past have been seen and documented by unimpeachable sailors and explorers. Some of these disappearing and appearing islands are playing their tricks today. As G. C. Henderson has written, "Though the information given by the commanders in their charts and logbooks may be at frequent variance with actual fact, it is nevertheless a true account of what they saw."

For many of the E.D. islands have been real. A small isle, for instance, may have existed for a while and then disappeared in the deluge following some seismic disturbances under the water or shiftings on the ocean floor. After every earthquake and tremor, there are repercussions in the ocean. Often the water is merely reclaiming an island it had lent to the surface for a while.

Another possibility is that the land sighted was really a "floating island." It might be a huge clump of water vegeta-

tion that appears and disappears in season. In the Arctic and Antarctic areas icebergs and huge ice formations are often mistaken for islands. These "ice islands" sometimes have rocks and earth on their surfaces, and even fresh water ponds with mosses. Such floating islands are important because they sometimes carry an entire chunk of animal and plant life from one area of the world to another, transforming the ecology of our planet.

As early as the days of ancient Greece, floating islands appeared in myth and legend. Delos was thought to have been such an island wandering up and down the Aegean Sea until Zeus tethered it to the ocean bottom. Such a tale might easily have had a basis in fact. Floating islands can be found today all over the world. Often they are seen in the Indian Ocean. Several years ago, a U.S. destroyer escort, steaming south of Cuba, sighted a small round island. It was complete with ten trees. However, a day later, when a botanist and entomologist were flown out to explore the island, it was missing—either attached to another, more solid piece of land by then, or sunk.

Still another possibility is that some islands can be made— or unmade—by man. Sir Thomas Browne pointed all this out in the seventeenth century. "Islands," he wrote, "were not from the beginning, that many have been made by Art, that some Isthmuses have been eaten through by the Sea, and others cut by the Spade."

And of course, to add to Sir Thomas' list, some islands might not have been islands at all, but optical illusions caused by the horizon line stretched shimmering between sea and sky. A black cloudbank, patches of seaweed, a dead whale, derelict ships, ocean scum floating on the top of water—any of these could be mistaken at a distance for an island, a shoal, or a piece of solid land. But they might be recorded in the logbook as a real island, a true account of what the captain saw.

Some of the disappearing islands have been real. Some have been mistakes. And some have been only dreams. Here are a few marked E.D. or P.D. on maps. Decide for yourself.

Chapter 10

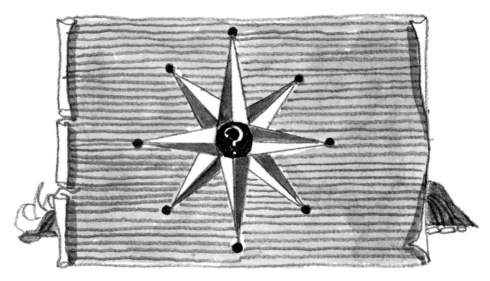

E. D.-Existence Doubtful

FALCON ISLAND: E.D.

Supposedly in the Pacific, off the coast of the Tongan Islands, Falcon Island was first sighted in 1864 by the captain of the *H. M. S. Falcon*. The captain reported the island as an unmarked shoal and a hazard to navigation.

Twelve years later, a British warship in the vicinity maneuvered carefully around the area because of the marked shoal, but found nothing there. All that could be seen at the supposed site of Falcon Island was a thin column of smoke rising up out of the sea. The ship cruised back and forth near the column and, while the crew watched in fascination, the island was born again! With a splendid belching of smoke and flame, there was a vol-

canic eruption that spewed up a piece of the earth from
the sea. And when the newly reborn island was measured, it rose 290 feet above the water.

The captain of the warship hurried back to report his
find and the new island was rechristened Falcon Island.
Four years later, a British geologist named Lister came to
examine the baby island. It was not a healthy child. The
sea had reclaimed much of the land, and what was left
rose only 153 feet above the waterline.

By 1895, the sickly child-island rose only 40 feet high.
And on its thirteenth birthday, the island vanished alto-
gether, leaving behind only the original small shoal.

But that was not the end of Falcon Island. In 1927, it
was miraculously born again, almost a hundred feet high.
Then Tongan officials sailed immediately to the spot and
planted the Tongan flag on the topmost point of the island. The flag still waves bravely—until next time.

ST. BRENDAN'S ISLAND: E.D.

If the weather is clear and you are very lucky, you might
sight St. Brendan's from one of the Canary Islands. The
Canary Islanders swear that it exists. They say it is moun-
tainous, ninety leagues in length. Yet they also say it is
only seen in intervals, for it is an earthly paradise, and not
many are saintly enough to be allowed to live there. In
fact, so it is said, the few expeditions that actually landed
on the island were all met with the volcanic wrath of the
desecrated holy isle.

It has been a holy island ever since St. Brendan and his
six companions, all bishops, took refuge there from the
murdering Moors in the first half of the sixth century.
They easily recognized the island as a holy one because
of the "trains of angels rising from it." Each founded a
city on the tiny island.

This mysterious St. Brendan's is actually on some maps, for expeditions that set out to discover it have claimed some measure of success. But the island has been variously identified as part of the Canaries, part of the Madeiras, part of the Azores, or west of the Cape Verde group. (And to further confuse things, other islands have since been called after the saint, such as one off the coast of Newfoundland.)

In 1570, the Portuguese explorer Pedro Vello declared that his ship put ashore on St. Brendan's because of a storm. The sailors saw a stream that meandered into a wooded valley. Reaching the stream, they saw giant footsteps on the bank, some thirty-six inches long. When several of the sailors, hungry for fresh meat, started to hunt a herd of sheep they saw wandering near the woods, a storm suddenly blew up. Vello and the rest of his men ran for the ship, and no sooner did they get aboard than the island—with the erstwhile hunters—disappeared.

Another Latin sailor, Marcos Verde, also chanced upon the island. He decided to cut down a tree to prove he

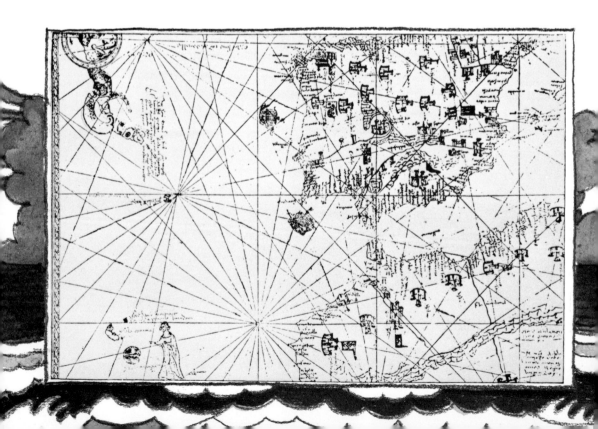

had been there. But as soon as his axe bit into the trunk, a storm arose of such supernatural force that he and his men were forced to race for their ship. The ship and the men were swept out to sea by the storm. When they returned to try again, the island seemed to have vanished. They never rediscovered it.

However, a third Portuguese explorer landed on St. Brendan's and, forcing his way up the steep slippery slope of black rock, managed to reach the island's summit. There he prepared to bore a hole in which to insert the Portuguese flag so that he could claim the island for his king. No sooner had his men started boring the hole than "blood-red liquid" began to pour from it. An "earthquake" rocked the island and, as the men reached their ship in terror, the island erupted in fire and smoke and sank from sight.

The last recorded expedition to St. Brendan's was in October 1721. This time, Captain Don Gaspar de Dominguez took no chances. He approached the island with two holy friars and some holy water. He and his men landed in safety and departed in same. But they never found the island again.

Since then, the island has occasionally been "seen" by holy men, by three blind men, and by mystics in dreams. But whether or not what they "saw" was real, and whether the Portuguese explorers were all exaggerating what occurred, is still open to debate.

DOUGHERTY ISLAND: E.D.

In 1800, an American whaling captain, Captain Swain out of Nantucket, sighted a heretofore unmarked island at Latitude 59° S, Longitude 90–100° W. He wrote in his logbook that the island was covered with ice, snow, birds, and seals, and was approximately eight miles long and eighty feet high. He called it after himself, Swain's Island.

The land was sighted again a few years later by two other New England sailors, and one, Captain Macy (also of Nantucket) claimed that the water around the island was "dark-colored and containing much rockweed and kelp."

Yet scarcely thirty years later, when two American vessels set out specifically to explore Swain's Island, it could not be found.

Then, in 1841, Captain Dougherty of the whaler *James Stewart* passed by the island at three hundred yards and kept it in sight for over a day. Captain Dougherty recorded the newly rediscovered island as Latitude 59°20′ S, Longitude 120°20′ W. He described it in detail and, of course, named it after himself—Dougherty Island.

His discovery was confirmed in 1885, 1886, 1890, and 1893. In fact, when in 1893 a New England ship sailed around it, the captain reported that the island was utterly

King *Arthur* and his valiant Knights of the Round *Table.*
Sir Triftram. *Sir* Launcelot. *Sir* Galahad. *Sir* Perciuall.
Sir Gauwin. *Sir* Ector. *Sir* Bors. *Sir* Lionell. *Sir* Griflet.
Sir Gaheris. *Sir* Tor. *Sir* Acolon. *Sir* Ewaine. *Sir* Marhaus.
Sir Pelleas *Sir* Sagris. *Sir* Turquine. *Sir* Kay. *Sir* Gareth.

Sir Beaumans. *Sir* Berſunt. *Sir* Palamide. *Sir* Beleobus.
Sir Ballamore. *Sir* Galohalt. *Sir* Lamarcke. *Sir* Floll.

desolate and that there was nothing else near it for more than a thousand miles.

The following year, 1894, and on all other occasions, the island was missing. A research vessel, the *Ruapehu*, searched for it four separate times. Where once an island surrounded by rockweed and kelp lay anchored in the ocean, there was nothing for miles around. When recent ships passed over its position and took soundings, it was proven that there was nothing but water for three miles down.

In 1932, Dougherty Island, originally called Swain's, was stricken from the charts of the world.

AVALON: E.D.

In Britain there is an enduring belief in King Arthur and his Knights of the Round Table. According to the story—or history, depending upon your beliefs—Arthur knew he was dying. And so he went with the fey Morgana to the fairy island of Avalon to be healed of his wounds. He promised his supporters that when he was well again he would return to rule England forever. He was never seen again.

The fairy island of Avalon, by tradition, was identified with the lake isle of Avalon where, in medieval times, a monastery was built. In 1193, the monks, who then dwelt upon the lake isle, discovered graves in the cemetery that they were convinced belonged to Arthur and Guinevere. (This discovery insured that many pious travelers would stop by the island monastery on tours and thus help keep the monastery coffers filled!)

According to medieval accounts, the king and queen had been entombed in a hollow oak in the Celtic—or Druidic—manner. A cross served as a marker for the grave. On it was the inscription: HIC JACET SEPUL-TUS INCLITUS REX ARTHURIUS IN INSULA

AVALONIA, Here lies buried the renowned King Arthur in the island of Avalon.

The monks discovered in the hollow oak the bones of a
man and a woman. And a tress of hair was also entombed
in the tree, the strands still long and golden. But the minute
one monk reached out to touch the golden strands, they
turned to dust.

The bodies were supposedly reinterred in a new church
that was built to hallow the spot. But bones, grave oak,
cross, and all disappeared long ago. And where the lake
isle of Avalon was once—an island in the midst of a marsh
—there is today only an intricate system of ditches and
drains that keep the swampy land dry. Whether the
monastery island was also the fairy isle of Avalon, nobody
knows for sure.

BUSS ISLAND: E.D.

In 1578, a small three-masted ship known as a ."buss"
sailed with a fleet of fifteen other ships to find the elusive
Northwest Passage. They sailed all the way to the Hudson
Strait. The captain of the fleet was Martin Frobisher.

The buss, the *Emmanuel of Bridgewater*, was separated
from its sister ships on the return trip because of bad
weather. She found herself in the mouth of a rocky bay
on Baffin Island (north of Canada's Quebec) now known
as Frobisher Bay. Slowly, the buss made her way alone
across the North Atlantic towards England. At Latitude
58° N, she all but rammed into a tiny uncharted island.
It was an admirable stopping point for the exhausted crew,
and they stayed overnight.

The island, according to the narrative of the journey,
was "fruitful, full of woods, and a champion countrie."

But to this day, the island has never been sighted—much
less landed upon—again.

LYONESSE: E.D.

Off the tip of Cornwall in England, where the land slopes down to the sea and cliffs drop earth and rock down, down, down to the water below, lies the long-lost island of Lyonesse, said to have sunk beneath the waves.

The people of Cornwall talk of fishermen who sail the crystal waters and, peering over the sides of their boats, have seen the roofs of houses and church steeples under the sea. These fishermen swear they hear the long-drowned church bells toll warnings of an impending storm or disaster. And some have even reported seeing mermaids, their long green hair floating behind them, swimming in and out of the barnacled windows of the houses of the submerged town. Yet modern divers find nothing there to substantiate these tales or the story that Lyonesse sank one night. There was said to have been only one survivor of that cataclysm, a lad named Trevillon who had leaped upon a horse and ridden furiously ahead of the all-engulfing surf, reaching the mainland safely. Trevillon is long dead, and his story cannot be verified, but the Cornish folk believe it is true.

BRAZIL E.D.

A few hundred miles west of Southern Ireland lay a green and flourishing island, according to the Angelino Dulcert map of 1325. The island, variously called Brazil, Breasil, Brasil, Brasylle, and Berzil, was described for six hundred years as either a single circular island or a ring of green and flourishing islands, so beautiful in fact that its name combined two Irish Gaelic words: *Breas* and *ail*, "superbly fine."

In 1452, 1482, and 1498 numerous expeditions were made to discover the island. The merchants of England were anxious to find the land, for it was believed that the island was the site of a mountain that yielded dye. (The word *brasil* was also related to the word in French and Spanish for coal, a material used in dying cloth.)

However, it wasn't until John Nisbet, an Irish sea captain, sailed into Killibega Harbor in 1674, that anyone actually claimed to have landed on the green isle. He described the island as inhabited by giant black rabbits and by a magician who had kept several Scottish castaways captive in his spellbound castle.

Until the nineteenth century, Brazil was marked on the maps of the British Admiralty, though it had shrunk by all accounts into nothing more than Brazil Rock. When the British finally removed it from their charts, only the legend remained.

DAVIS LAND: E.D.

In 1687, while escaping from pursuing warships, the Dutch pirate John Davis and his crew on the *Bachelor's Delight* came upon an island five hundred miles west of South America. It was a lovely and lonely place, with "a long sandy beach and coconut palms."

Captain Davis even recorded its latitude as 20°27' S.

Another island, about twelve leagues to the west, was also recorded, with high peaks rising majestically out of the water.

The pirates had no time to land, however, for the warships were too close behind.

The island remained on charts of the sea for fifty years as Davis Land. But no one else ever found it.

Forty years later, while searching for the mysterious Davis Land, Dutch Captain Roggeveen discovered Easter Island, site of an even larger mystery.

Davis land was finally removed from the charts in 1935.

HUNTER ISLAND: E.D.

Sailing to latitude 15°31′ S, longitude 176°11′ W, Captain Hunter of the *Donna Carmelite* came upon a perfect island in 1823. It was a tropical paradise with fertile fields and both coconut and breadfruit growing wild.

This island was already inhabited, according to Hunter's story, by very intelligent Polynesians.

The natives had a curious trait by which they could be recognized. Each child, at birth, had the little finger of the left hand amputated at the second joint.

Only Captain Hunter ever visited Hunter Island—or *Onaneuse*, as it was called by its natives. It has never been seen again.

FEMINA: E.D.

Near Martinique, Christopher Columbus sought the island of Femina, the legendary Isle of Women. All the women on Femina were said to be tall, young, and ex-

tremely beautiful. They sang as sweetly as the ancient sirens, calling to passing ships.

The crews of any ships that landed on the island were allowed three months of fruit, honey, and love. At the end of that time, the sailors were rudely thrust back on board their ships.

Columbus never found this sailors' paradise, and needless to say, no one else has, either.

GREEN ISLAND: E.D.

Every seven years, an island used to rise in the sea between Ireland's Rathland and Bengore Isles. It was a green and rich island, marked as latitude 44°48′ N, and longitude 26°10′ W. Irish sailors viewing it through their spyglasses have reported the island as a fine land adorned with woods and lawns. They could even discern on it a country fair, with people selling yarn and other wares.

Yet Green Island has never been landed upon and, in 1853, it disappeared as well from the maps of the world.

There are hundreds of similar phantom islands: the Auroras, a group of three islands said to be in the South Atlantic; the Royal Company Islands near Tasmania; Pacific islands called Bunker, New, Sultan, Eclipse, Roca; South Pacific islands of Spraque, Monks, Favorite, Duke of York, Little Paternoster, Massacre and Mortlock.

Do these islands exist? Were they merely the map-makers' dreams? Or will they reappear in the future?

They are some of the mysteries left in the world.

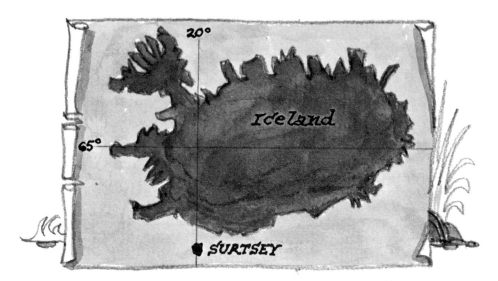

Chapter 11

SURTSEY
Latitude: 63° N
Longitude: 20°

Birth of an Island

Islands that appear and disappear are certainly a part of the world's ocean legends. But in 1963, with the aid of cameras and scientific observers, some of those legends were given a solid basis of fact. For on November 14, 1963, a kind of miracle occurred. On that date, in full view of modern scientists, the ocean went into labor.

The result was the birth of an island.

In the waters of the North Atlantic near Iceland there have been many legends and many pseudo-scientific accounts of ocean marvels. In 1178, for example, a monk named Herbert of Clairvaux wrote *Liber Miraculorum*, the *Book of Wonders*. In it he said, ". . . frequently fire is seen to break with stupendous force out of the ocean high above the waves, burning fishes and all living things in the sea." Herbert was describing underwater explosions off the coast of Iceland, and he wrote with much more accuracy than he has been credited.

Fire at sea and boiling waters near Iceland's rugged coasts are not unique. And while it would seem the stuff of which legends are made, in this case such "miracles" are true. Iceland is near an underwater ridge that is full of volcanic activity. Scientists have estimated that in Iceland itself there are volcanic eruptions approximately once every five years.

Still, when on November 14, 1963 the fishing boat *Isleifur* sailed into waters that were roiling and rolling and foul with a sulphurous smell, the world had a hard time believing the miracle that was to occur. It was the first time that scientists were to be the watchful midwives at the unexpected birth of an underwater island.

First the engineer, then the captain, and at last the cook of the *Isleifur* were aware of the awful smell, the peculiar roll of the sea. But it was the cook who, at 7:30 A.M. first noticed the smoke. They thought there was a ship in trouble somewhere on the seas.

However, when the captain called a nearby radio station, he discovered that there were no SOS signals in the area. No ships in trouble. Yet if his binoculars were not lying, the black columns of smoke rising above the surface of the sea meant something. The captain, who was Icelandic, suspected volcanic activity.

By 8 A.M., the captain and his crew could see three separate eruption columns rising two hundred feet in the air. Captain Tomasson decided to move closer for a better look.

As the crew of the *Isleifur* watched, the black columns started ejecting stones and boulders. Then the columns began to emit flashes of light. Yet strangely enough, there was little noise. It was like being in the middle of a dream.

As long as the activity remained underwater, the eerie silence continued.

Near the ship the water temperature was nine degrees higher than it should have been. Soon airplanes, alerted by Captain Tomasson, circled the underwater volcano and its black columns, taking pictures.

Within four hours, geologists were on hand to witness the phenomenon. The scientific watch had begun.

By the time the first scientists arrived, the columns were 1200 feet high. By 3 P.M., the eruption columns were 1600 feet high, and the smoke itself had risen four miles. It could be seen from Reykjavik, the capital city of Iceland.

The sea around the erupting volcano was a peculiar color. Instead of a clear blue-green, it was brownish. The brownish sea was behaving peculiarly, too. Great waves were breaking where none had broken before. The reason was soon easy to see. A ridge of land was developing, just below the surface of the sea, where the volcano was smoking.

And the next night the island was born.

The island was sturdy from the beginning. Thirty-three

feet high on the second day of eruption, the small piece of land kept growing. By December 30, it was 415 feet high, having grown and receded daily; added to by the ash, cinders, and pumice of the ever-erupting volcano, cut through continually by the sea. But the island seemed to have stabilized by the end of January at 525 feet above sea level. Then it turned grey with snow.

All during its slow but steady growth, the island was bombarded with huge "lava bombs" that were hurled from the volcano. Some of these bombs were heaved as high as 3300 feet, crashing with loud *bangs* as they fell into the sea. For the island was no longer silent. Besides the noise of the bombs hitting the ocean, there was now a steady rumbling that accompanied the eruptions. Flashes of lightning lit up the eruptions' smoke clouds. Thunder barked for hours at a time. It was a cosmic light show.

On December 6, during one of the small lulls in the eruptions, when the clouds and vapors were blown away by the wind and the island came into view like a prima donna making an entrance, three Frenchmen landed on the island. These daredevils were sponsored by the French magazine *Paris-Match*. They had come by speedboat at the first sign of a lull. They managed to stay fifteen minutes before eruptions forced them to leave. (Their account reads a little like the stories of the St. Brendan's Island landings.)

Since the island had been landed upon, it was time for it to be named. The Icelandic Government turned over the task to their Place Names Committee. The Committee came up with *Surtsey*, named after the giant Surtur who, according to Norse legend, had brought fire to the cold northern countries from some warmer land far to the South. And the main volcano on Surtsey was called, appropriately, Surtur.

The second landing was effected by some people who

lived in the nearby Vestmann Islands. They liked neither the island's new name nor the fact that Iceland had taken over a part of their own chain of islands. So they visited Surtsey in order to place a sign with a different name on it. The name they chose was, unimaginatively, Vesturey, West Island.

But when they landed, Surtur, the volcano, began to pelt the islanders with pumice and mud. The Vestmann Islanders escaped gratefully, just as the sailors had who had tried to bore a hole for the flag on St. Brendan's Island.

On the third landing, scientists quickly collected samples of rock, both volcanic and non-volcanic stones that had come up with the island from the old ocean floor.

In February 1964, the island went into a round of furious volcanic activity, belching and coughing up so much material that it lengthened itself by one thousand feet. By April 4, Surtsey was 5600 feet long.

Then a new act unfolded. As if to announce it with a fanfare, Surtur sent up a column of fire five hundred feet high. A glowing river of red hot lava began to flow from the volcano's mouth, down its side to Surtsey's beaches. As the flow reached the shore, it spread out into many little fingers of red streams and each entered the sea with a hiss of white steam.

Lava flowed the entire month of April, day and night. On clear nights, the lava fires, glowing bright red against the midnight skies, could be seen for distances of almost two hundred miles.

When the lava flow ended, April was over, and Surtsey was measured again. The island was found to be over one-half mile square. And on August 25, the island reached its largest point—567 feet high, 1.3 miles long. That meant it was roughly two-thirds the size of New York City's Central Park.

Surtsey had become a scientist's dreamworld. Here they could watch first-hand as a new-made land was wind-worked and sea-carved. They could watch as the forces of nature changed and molded and shaped a virgin territory. They could record gentle slopes being cut by the surf into sheared-off cliffs. They could photograph lava spreading out and fissuring.

But they could do something even more exciting than that. As Sigurdur Thorarinsson, one of the geologists who spent a great deal of time on Surtsey wrote, "No land can be more completely devoid of life than a volcanic island that rises from the sea." Surtsey had been sterilized by fire and water. It offered the scientists a unique opportunity to study where, how, and in what order living organisms arose.

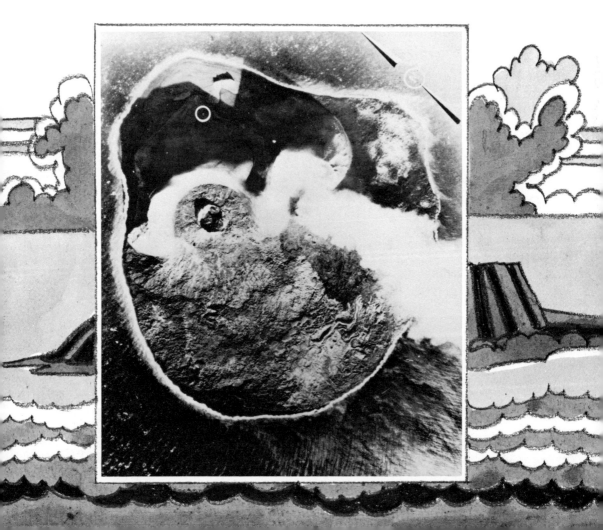

Surtsey was a natural laboratory.

So in April, once the explosive activities had stopped, the world's scientists began to make a series of visits to the lonely North Atlantic island. They came by boat, by airplane, and by helicopter. In May, Surtsey was declared a sanctuary to be restricted to scientists only. A year later, a small hut was built on the island to house the scientific headquarters. It could accommodate three to five men.

In the next few months the handful of scientists who labored on Surtsey were shaken when the volcano Surtur began to pour out lava again. The glowing red-hot river came within 120 yards of the hut while the men watched with fearful interest. But in four days, the lava stopped flowing again and the mountain, as if to signal that its activities were at an end, blew out a series of regular smoke rings.

The Surtur eruptions ended for good on June 5, 1967, having lasted three and a half years. By this time, the island of Surtsey contained 692 acres.

But even before the volcano had quieted, the first living organisms had arrived, unannounced and unheralded: the microbes. No one knows for sure when they first landed on Surtsey. But they were already there in considerable numbers when they were discovered on May 14, 1964, six months after Surtsey had surfaced. Some were apparently brought by gulls that had alighted on the island, during lulls between explosions, when the island was scarcely two weeks old. Others had been deposited by the waves on Surtsey's shores.

In April, redwings had found their way to the island. Soon the migratory birds had adopted it as a waystop on their long trips: the dunlins, the plovers, the snow buntings and others.

Then on June 7, 1964, the seals came aboard the island and adopted it for their own. Various other marine animals

drifted ashore, too, some to die on the island, others to make their way back to the sea—cuttlefish, Norway pout, and lumpfish were noted.

By the summer of 1964, flies and butterflies were seen on the island.

Nesting birds found Surtsey the following year. A few pair of kittiwakes nested in the lava cliffs.

Seeds began to drift ashore from the Icelandic coast, as did some living plants. On June 3, 1965, the first green plant was discovered on Surtsey. This first plant was a "sea rocket" that grows particularly well on Iceland's sandy south coast. Several sea rockets had been washed ashore in seaweed and had thrived in Surtsey's small sheltered lagoon. The island had changed from a barren sterile laboratory to a green land in only one and a half years.

What has the birth and development of Surtsey told us? Many things we now know and many things we hope to know. That islands that have disappeared and appeared in legend might have a solid basis in fact. That islands like the Vestmanns in Iceland arose in fire, smoke, and flame from the sea. How certain kinds of volcanos work. What happens on islands like the Galapagos where strange and rare creatures abound. And perhaps, too, it has given us some clues to the reappearance of life on Earth after the great glaciers had wiped the slate of life clean.

Surtsey was born in mystery and fire. In the old days it would have been thought that magic and wizardry were involved. But when the volcanic fires of Surtsey were banked, some of the mystery and surprise proved to be explainable in scientific terms. So it is with many "magical" things.

So may it be someday with all the wizard islands.

Notes on Illustrations

In addition to the original maps and drawings by Robert Quackenbush, maps, photographs, and other materials have been used from the following sources:

Page 56, 59, 60   Pictures of the giant sculptures on Easter Island (From the book AKU, AKU by Thor Heyerdahl, courtesy of *Rand McNally & Co.*)

Page 62   Hand colored etchings rendered at Easter Island in early 1800s (courtesy *New York Public Library*)

Page 64   Raising a giant sculpture on Easter Island. (From T. Heyerdahl, op. cit., courtesy of *Rand McNally & Co.*)

Page 68   Engraving of Darwin with turtle (*Bettmann Archive*)

Page 70   "Living fossils," cacti unique to the Galapagos Islands (courtesy Erna R. Eisendrath)

Page 71   Hand colored etchings rendered ca. 1847 of Indian man and woman (courtesy *New York Public Library*)

Page 72   Group of sea iguanas on Albermarle in the Galapagos group (Wide World Photos)

Page 88   Section of Pizigani map of 1367, showing Saint Brendan in lower Left-hand corner (courtesy *The Viking Press*)

Page 90   King Arthur at the Roundtable, woodcut frontispiece from THE HISTORY OF PRINCE ARTHUR, 1634 (courtesy *New York Public Library*)

Page 96   Double-tailed Spanish Siren. Print by Juan Joffre, Valencia, 1520 (courtesy *New York Public Library*)

Page 100   The now tranquil isle of Surtsey (courtesy *Icelandic Airlines*)

Page 103   Aerial view of Surtsey (courtesy *Wide World Photos*)

Page 104   Lava eruption on Surtsey, August 1966. Photograph by Wm. A. Keith (courtesy *Iceland Tourist Bureau*)

For Further Reading

Islands in General

de la Mare, Walter. *Desert Islands & Robinson Crusoe.* New York, Farrar & Rinehart, 1930.

Manley, Seon & Robert. *Islands: Their Lives, Legends & Lore.* Philadelphia, Chilton, 1970.

Selsam, Millicent. *Birth of an Island.* New York, Scholastic Publications, 1959.

Appledore & Smuttynose

Drake, Samuel Adams. *A Book of New England Legends & Folklore.* Boston, Robert Brothers, 1884.

Hilly, Ralph Nading. *Yankee Kingdoms: Vermont & New Hampshire.* New York, Harper & Row, 1960.

Leighton, Oscar. *Ninety Years at the Isles of Shoals.* Andover, Mass., Andover Press, 1929.

Rich, L. D. *State O' Maine.* New York, Harper & Row, 1964.

————. *The Coast of Maine.* New York, Thomas Y. Crowell, 1956.

Rutledge, Lyman. *The Isles of Shoals in Lore & Legend.* Barre, Vermont, Barre Press, 1965.

Simpson, Dorothy. *The Maine Islands in Story & Legend.* Philadelphia, Lippincott, 1960.

Snow, Edward Rowe. *Secrets of the Atlantic Islands.* New York, Dodd, Mead, 1950.

————. *True Tales of Buried Treasure.* New York, Dodd, Mead, 1962.

Young, Hazel. *Islands of New England.* Boston, Little, Brown, 1954.

Atlantis

Carter, Lin (editor). *The Magic of Atlantis.* New York, Lancer Books, 1970.

Cayce, Edgar. *Edgar Cayce on Atlantis.* New York, Paperback Library, 1968.

de Camp, L. Sprague. *Lost Continents.* New York, Dover Publications, 1954.

Donnelly, Ignatius. *Atlantis: The Antediluvian World.* New York, Steiner Publications, 1971.

Luce, J. V. *New Light on an Old Legend.* New York, McGraw-Hill, 1969.

Easter Island

Dos Passos, John. *Easter Island: Island of Enigmas.* New York, Doubleday, 1971.

Englert, Father Sebastian. *Island at the Center of the World*. New York, Scribners, 1970.

Heyerdahl, Thor. *Aku-Aku*. New York, Pocket Books, 1958.

Von Daniken, Erich. *Chariots of the Gods*. New York, Bantam Books, 1970.

The Galapagos

Brower, Kenneth (editor). *Galapagos: The Flow of Wildness, Vols. 1 & 2*. New York, Sierra Club/Ballantine Books, 1970.

Darwin, Charles. *The Voyage of the* Beagle. New York, Bantam Books, 1958.

Friedlander, Paul, J. C. "Galapagos: A Return to Life's Earliest Beginnings;" *The New York Times*, February 15, 1970.

Mindlin, Helen Mather-Smith. *Strange Animals*. New York, Bobbs-Merrill, 1962.

George's Island

Snow, Edward Rowe. *Secrets of the Atlantic Islands*. New York, Dodd, Mead, 1950.

———. *The Islands of Boston Harbor*. Andover, Mass., Andover Press, 1936.

Isle of Man

Scott, Sir Walter. *Pevril of the Peak*.

John's Island

Rich, L. D. *The Coast of Maine*. New York, Thomas Y. Crowell, 1956.

Young, Hazel. *Islands of New England*. Boston, Little, Brown, 1954.

Sable Island

Snow, Edward Rowe. *Mysteries & Adventures Along the Atlantic Coast*. New York, Dodd, Mead, 1960.

Surtsey

Thorarinsson, Siggurdur. *Surtsey*. New York, Viking, 1964.

Vanishing Islands

Bodger, Joan. *How the Heather Looks*. New York, Viking, 1965.

Gaddis, Vincent. *Invisible Horizons*. New York, Ace Books, 1965.

Hall, Mr. and Mrs. S. C. *Ireland, Its Scenery, Character, Etc., Volume 3*. London, Jeremiah How, 1843.

Hurwood, Bernhardt. *The Second Occult Review Reader*. New York, Award Books, 1969.

Manley, Seon & Robert. *Islands: Their Lives, Legends & Lore*. Philadelphia, Chilton, 1970.

Miller, Helen Hill. *The Realms of Arthur*. New York, Scribners, 1969.

Ramsay, Raymond H. *No Longer on the Map*. New York, Viking, 1972.

Index

ABOUT THE AUTHOR

JANE YOLEN has a storyteller's natural interest in folk-tales, which led her to the discovery of the ghost stories in this collection. Fascinated by the fact that so many ghosts seemed to be associated with islands, she found as she did further research that many islands also had natural, scientific mysteries as intriguing as the supernatural ones; both fact and fancy are represented in this book.

Versatile author of many distinguished works of fiction, Jane Yolen is equally well known for factual books such as *Friend*, a biography of the Quaker George Fox, and *World on a String: The Story of Kites*, chosen as a Notable Book by the American Library Association. A graduate of Smith College, she worked for a while as an editor of books for young people, but now devotes herself to writing, teaching, and running a busy household. She and her husband have three young children; they live in a lovely old farmhouse in Hatfield, Massachusetts.

ABOUT THE ARTIST

ROBERT QUACKENBUSH was born in California and brought up in Arizona. He is a graduate of the Art Center College of Design in Los Angeles. Mr. Quackenbush now lives in New York City but spends much of his time on painting excursions in Europe and the United States. He has illustrated more than fifty books for children and adults, for which he has received honors and citations from the Society of Illustrators and the American Institute of Graphic Arts. His work has been exhibited at leading museums throughout the country, including the Philadelphia Academy of Fine Arts and the Whitney Museum in New York City, and at his own gallery in New York, where he also teaches art.

Santa Clara County
LIBRARY

Renewals:

(800) 471-0991
www.santaclaracountylib.org